MW00856478

Martyrdom Street

Martyrdom Street

Firoozeh Kashani-Sabet

SYRACUSE UNIVERSITY PRESS

Copyright © 2010 by Syracuse University Press

Syracuse, New York, 13244-5290

All Rights Reserved

First Edition 2010

10   11   12   13   14   15   6   5   4   3   2   1

"Martyrdom Street" appeared in *A World Between,* edited by M. Khorrami and Persis Karim (1999),
and is reprinted with the permission of George Braziller Publishers. "The Sand Castle" appeared
in *Let Me Tell You Where I've Been,* edited by Persis Karim (2006).

∞ The paper used in this publication meets the minimum requirements
of the American National Standard for Information Sciences—Permanence
of Paper for Printed Library Materials, ANSI Z39.48-1992.

For a listing of books published and distributed by Syracuse University Press,
visit our Web site at SyracuseUniversityPress.syr.edu.

ISBN: 978-0-8156-0975-9

Library of Congress Cataloging-in-Publication Data

Kashani-Sabet, Firoozeh, 1967–

Martyrdom street / Firoozeh Kashani-Sabet. — 1st ed.

p. cm.

ISBN 978-0-8156-0975-9 (cloth : alk. paper)

1. Women—Iran—Fiction.   2. Iranians—United States—Fiction.

3. Iranian American women—Fiction.   4. Self-realization in women—Fiction.

5. Iran—History—1979–1997—Fiction.   I. Title.

PS3611.A7853M37 2010

813'.6—dc22   2010003599

Manufactured in the United States of America

To the Javaheri children—my "jewels"—with love from Mommy

Firoozeh Kashani-Sabet teaches Middle Eastern history and directs the Middle East Center at the University of Pennsylvania. Born and raised in Tehran, Iran, Dr. Kashani-Sabet has traveled extensively throughout Europe and the Middle East and speaks several languages. She enjoys Persian cuisine and treasures her Gilaki heritage.

Contents

Acknowledgments

Writing this book has spanned more than a decade. The editorial and production teams at Syracuse University Press—Mary Selden Evans, Lynn Hoppel, Marcia Hough, and Lisa Renee Kuerbis—could not have been more enthusiastic and professional in preparing the manuscript for publication. Thanks very much, ladies!

Friends and cousins have generously shared their words of wisdom and offered much-needed love and kindness. I gratefully acknowledge the support of Susan Amin, Soussan Azimi-Sanavi, Mansur Bavar, Adrienne Defendi, Matthew Greenfield, Nicole Samii Holdener, and Roxanne Samii Brown.

The curiosity and love of my nieces, Leila and Sara Kashani-Sabet, inspired me to keep at it and to finish the book. Girls, "Ammeh" really appreciates it! To my husband, Alireza Javaheri, I owe the greatest debt of gratitude for his unconditional support of my writing and career. You're the best! Finally, to my children, God bless you! Nothing would have been possible without you.

Martyrs and Prophets

From the shrines of Parsa
rise the dust of ages
and the murmurs of
hidden faces.

In this hall of wanderers,
where winds swallow their whispers,
Parsa's martyrs and prophets
scorn the long shadows
cast upon the royal gateway
fearing the day

when the earth shall tremble
and the hidden
shall unveil their faces,
rising against tyranny.

Martyrdom Street

Prologue

Nasrin

It happened by chance. I was in the basement, away from all the mayhem on the street. My eyes followed a cockroach scurrying into an empty classroom where a book lay on some dusty boxes. As the roach crawled onto its frayed pages, he touched my hand bearing down on his antennae, and instinct directed him to a corner between the boxes and the wall. At last, the collection of poetry was in my hands.

At first glance, the poetry book, like the classroom I'd stepped into, seemed of little interest except maybe to a cockroach. The leather binding, once fastened to the sheets with gold thread, was falling apart. The brown watermarks bordering the margins washed away dark secrets scripted in fine calligraphy. At the slightest human touch, morsels of yellowed paper chipped off the edges of the title page where someone had inscribed a verse in poor Persian. What was it that attracted me to the book? Was it the seduction of filth, the scent of decadence, or the security of immortality?

I found a seat on the floor and began to read. Alongside miniature portraits of naked women, I found stories of Parsa's prophets recited in the mystical language of a medieval prayer book. I didn't hear anybody calling my name, although later others would claim that they'd tried to find me. I didn't make much of the light tremors beneath my feet or the vapor that had infiltrated the building. In the poet's mysterious landscape, I saw stone columns sway unsteadily in the wind. I heard the cries of female warriors, the laments of weary mystics, and I saw myself among them.

As high flames swallowed the hall of wanderers, I read out loud, the way an old dervish had once taught me to recite sacred verses. That must have been why the soldiers found me in the room. Even then, I didn't stop reading. Who are you? they asked. I didn't answer. They pointed a gun to my face and grabbed the poetry book out of my hand. It's mine, I yelled. You shouldn't be reading this, they said. A soldier started to tear up its pages.

I don't know what came over me. The men meant no physical harm, but I felt the urge to run. Maybe it was the sight of strangers in a space so familiar. Maybe it was the movement of their guns. I grabbed the remainder of the poetry collection from the soldier's hands and hurried outside the building. When I approached the school gate, I sped into the crowd, my head down and the book still under my arm. I ran fast, behind antique shops and busy side streets, past gas stations and baqalis, with no volition of my own, just following the veiled faces around me. A young boy about my age offered me a handgun while another waved a white banner with Qur'anic adages. "Neither East nor West," they yelled, running faster toward Martyrdom Street. I started yelling, too, not revolutionary slogans but dissonant verses. As my voice melted into theirs, a woman grabbed the poetry collection out of my hands, and we fell to the ground, listening.

It could have been anybody. Guns were passed back and forth that day, and within minutes a rapid succession of shots muffled our raw voices. I found the woman at the doorstep of a bakery and wrapped a cloth around her hip to stop the rush of blood. Where are your parents? she asked. I don't know, I said. She tried to talk but drifted into sleep. I opened the front window of the bakery and waited at the entrance for five minutes or maybe an hour. When the bakers, the ambulances, the neighbors, and the police refused to arrive, I took her to the hospital myself. I waited there until the nurse wheeled her into the emergency room and bandaged her wound. Then I took the poetry collection and returned home. After the regime changed hands, our school was shut down. Nobody knows what happened to the neat stack of books, erasers, or pens. Nobody knows where all the teachers and students fled. At night, I see their hollow faces as shadows in the sky.

Burnt Leaves

Fatemeh

Red tulips are spring flowers, the flowers of carnage and carnal pleasure, the sins of wine and war brought together. The tulips in my garden grow in color-coordinated patches, like the ones in Tehran's Behest-e Zahra cemetery. I can almost hear them now, whispering to each other, the purple blossoms and the white buds, about marigolds, worms, and forgotten rebels. The yellow hyacinth, its sugary smell floating overhead, lives on for that man outside the post office. Or the pink tulips planted months after the accident. The brawls in the streets, the ardor in people's eyes, the stray cat in the neighborhood. I see them all here in nature's canvas. Instead of pastels, I choose vivid colors that would clash terribly on white burlap but that blend well under the sun. Colors that scream out against private indignities. Colors that capture lost innocence. Colors that live on long after the people are gone.

During the warm winters of Tehran, the tulips remain in full bloom. Today, they stiffen slightly under the unusual chill. I water them and the stink of manure rises just as the water touches the soil. Then I watch the puddles swell and empty around a cucumber bush. Swell and empty. Swell and empty. Swell and empty. My neighbor enters the garden without invitation and steps on a bed of petunias. She wants me to go with her to Darakeh, a nearby mountain resort. "Is Muhsin working today?" Shirin asks, referring to my husband. I pretend not to hear her. She stares at my face and then insists that I need to get out more. More? More what? More where? Just more, she says.

We drive to the outskirts of the city. The Damavand Mountains, with salted peaks and hollow valleys, cradle the capital on dark winter days. Somewhere toward the top of the ridge, where cars and motorcycles of ancient vintage are parked behind one another, we get out. Someone offers us tea, another fresh walnuts in a jar. A young man, the owner of a kebab stand, lights the fire to roast his marinated lamb chops and tomatoes. We walk and walk along a narrow passageway until we reach a wide flatland. Out there, where nature is gentle and expansive, families spread out their plastic tablecloths and sit around to drink freshly brewed tea with homemade sour cherry jam. Shirin buys two chicken kebab sandwiches wrapped in warm lavash bread. I find an empty corner to sit, but she yanks my arm, dragging me toward the road. "What's the matter?" I ask. Then I turn around and see Muhsin laughing with his young bride and eighteen-month-old baby boy. They don't see me. He dips a sugar cube in his tea, coughs wildly, and strokes his other wife. He was supposed to be at work again, supervising a construction site.

We tread to the top of the ridge, away from the cruelty of the moment. There are no lovers here today secretly sharing a moment of affection. Shirin removes her veil for a naughty second to catch the wind in her shiny black locks. "Don't you miss the wind blowing in your hair?" she asks. From the summit, where Shirin and I are standing, the men and women below seem to mingle naturally, laughing, no longer separated by artificial laws and social barriers. I take off my veil, too, to feel the air tickle my head. A crisp breeze wafts through my curls, and I shake my head softly at first, and then violently until I lose my step. I feel light and reach for a tree to steady myself.

As two men approach the parking lot, we quickly cover our heads and walk toward the car. The men are roughly the same age as Afsaneh's twenty-year-old son. They pass by our car as we eat our soggy chicken kebabs quietly in the back seat. On the way back, Shirin takes a detour off the expressway and drives past our old school, a landmark founded by American missionaries a hundred or so years earlier. At first, the school was open only to Armenian girls, but eventually Muslim families decided to send their daughters there as well. We were among the first class of Muslim girls. When we graduated, they published our pictures in the local newspaper, and our transitory fame helped us to win "good" husbands after graduation. Good husbands. Men who provided for their families, crowd-pleasers, and who occasionally slept with other women. By then, polygamy had fallen out of fashion.

∞

A street vendor sells fresh pomegranate juice outside the entrance to the school. On the west side of Martyrdom Street, we recognize the high walls encircling the campus. "Don't you want to go inside just one more time?" Shirin probes. Before hearing my answer, she rolls down her window and approaches the gatekeeper. She lies to him about having a son in the school. But the bearded guard refuses to let us through and quietly sips his tea. Finally, Shirin gives him a one-thousand-toman bill, and he lifts the chain to make way for our car.

We drive around the main circle and park the car behind the cafeteria. Past the swings and the soccer field, behind the old classrooms and the kiosk, there is the cherry tree. From my classroom window, I'd stare at its sprawling shadow, imagining the gardener who had planted its seed. I heard the rains that watered its roots. I saw my classmates climb up its thick trunk. I watched its long branches repel trespassers. Today, it stands even taller, having weathered a revolution and a war. A narrow road runs behind the cherry tree and leads to a back alley. It was here that I found the janitor's wife lying naked with the gardener. They did not see me. Lush green leaves were camouflaging my body. It was here behind the cherry tree that Shirin would secretly meet the man who became her husband.

We wander around for a few minutes, knowing our intrusion is safe now that the school is out for the day. Shirin pulls a small twig off the cherry tree as a keepsake. I feel the dusty sand covering the soccer field that was once a grassy meadow. There is little money for maintaining the grounds now that the school is run by religious seminarians. We walk past the soccer field and up the alley to leave the gates of the school. As we approach the top of the hill, two vintage Volkswagens swerve by, loudly honking their horns. A woman thrusts her head out the back window and hurls political leaflets. Then the front door flies open, and someone flings firebombs onto the road. Shirin pulls me back and we run in the direction of the soccer field. We squat and watch the flames roll down the hill that towers above the schoolyard. The gatekeeper, two turbaned men, and a young boy assemble within minutes but don't see us hiding behind the science building. Once the fires are tamed, they put up a chain to block the rear entrance. We wait until it's almost dark before venturing out. Two fallen lampposts block the sidewalk as we approach the car. The leaflets, now no more than inoffensive dust, powder the alley. And the cherry tree, once a stalwart warden, has virtually burned to the ground. The tree was a natural protector. A perennial father. God. But rebels don't know natural law.

A gardener waters a string of pansies next to the sanctuary, despite the drought, but nobody seems to mind. In the courtyard a mother rocks her infant son and hums a gentle lullaby. The baby stares into the distance, through the massive columns and their plaster moldings. When the humming stops and the preacher's voice rises, the infant shifts in his mother's arms and wails. "Maybe he's hungry," someone remarks. "Or tired," another surmises. Someone offers the woman bread and cheese. But the baby keeps crying and nobody knows what he needs. Even babies born after the twenty-second of Bahman dream of better times. Exasperated, the mother packs her bags and moves away. I don't remember Nasrin this way. She smiled at strangers and delighted at family outings.

On the path leading to the memorial, pieces of a ripped poster of the turbaned preacher are strewn in a corner, but no one bothers to pick them up. I step inside the Imam's shrine and walk toward the mausoleum. The smell of rosewater permeates the handwoven rugs on the floor. Next to me, a woman wails and kisses the iron grids that protect the Imam's tomb, asking for miracles. I try hard to imitate her piety but can't. Her crying makes me nervous and I decide to leave. Outside, a security guard approaches and removes his shoes by the entrance to the shrine. Today, he's only an ornament here. He does not see the teenage girl and boy flirt while sharing a bowl of pistachios. The girl's veil slowly slides down her head, exposing thick black curls, but nobody chastens her. The price of bread went up another ten tomans; the price of gasoline another five.

People don't care about ceremonies any more. Every holiday is an occasion for collective catharsis instead of a cause for celebration. Families congregate more for the sake of companionship than for politics. Even the twenty-second of Bahman—the anniversary of our revolution—is no exception. It's just another holiday, like the commemorations of Imams or the birthdays of kings. Despite the display of bright flashing lights in the trees and the propaganda of overhead banners, pedestrians ignore the revolutionary message. They listen instead to local candidates running for parliamentary elections.

Burnt Leaves

Zaynab, a twenty-something-year-old political candidate, boasts a pedigreed lineage that connects her to the leading religious folk in the country. Before she can finish, a hunchbacked man pelts her with roasted pumpkin seeds. He tells Zaynab about his granddaughter who at sixteen washes floors every day to help pay the rent for the one room he occupies with five other relatives in the slums of southern Tehran. I know Zaynab as a childhood friend of my daughter's. Zaynab promises to offer subsidized housing as part of her campaign. Her youthful optimism turns off the hunchback who walks away as she gives assurances. When Zaynab finishes her speech, she mingles with the crowd, eventually working her way to where I am standing near the bed of tulips. She kisses me and asks about my daughter, Nasrin, now living in the United States. I respond in a general way and wait for the conversation to move on to another topic. Nasrin and I won't talk again on the phone until the following week. I catch the next bus at the intersection and go home. My hand has started to ache, and I take some pills, waiting for today to spill into tomorrow. Muhsin is gone and will not return for hours. I won't remember him coming home.

Yasaman

The afternoon sun drops a shadow over his face. I don't hear them come in. What? Don't look! Don't look! Can he hear me? There. He smiles. The red puddle fills the flower patch. I poke him in the side. He lies there, silent, inside the red puddle that circles his hyacinths. Then one of the boys sets fire to the heap of dried leaves, and the smell of malice fills the neighborhood.

A breeze shakes the trees, and small twigs fall from the sky. I watch the red puddle by the hyacinths dry up in the sun. I don't know if anyone can smell the fire. Something in me aches, and I look for a place where I can go to abate the stinging in my stomach. As I walk past the deli, I stare at my reflection in the window, wondering when the bulges on my sides will disappear. Despite all the carrots and beets and celery and wheat, fat clings to my ribs. I've tried everything: diet, exercise, drinking eight glasses of water a day. I squat behind the trash bins. This will only take a minute. When I'm sure that nobody can see me, I bend over and force two fingers down my throat. I feel light.

Martyrdom Street

Across the coffee shop two workers dump a rake full of compost into a bonfire, reveling in its incineration. I'm sure they don't see me. I would recognize this burning stench anywhere. The first time I tried this, the smell of burnt leaves sailed through the half-open bathroom window. The odor lingered and I knew something inside me was decaying fast. I had to cleanse myself, at first once a day and then up to five times. I don't count any more.

Emerald Forests

Fatemeh

A tangle of figures—of three-legged cats, open coffins, and little girls' ribbons— takes shape in the white embossed porcelain coffee cup. Shirin observes the patterns as she prepares to tell my fortune. Maybe this is the way one pictures a city in the wake of a war or a flood. Or the way one abbreviates the suffering of a tribe for civilized company. But to Shirin, the coffee cup is a looking glass where she sees the kind face of kismet. She gingerly rotates the cup in her palm, staring intently at the patterns etched by the coffee stains, first with an air of puzzlement and then with purpose. "Do you see this?" she says, pointing to a thick hardened glob of ground coffee. I shake my head. She sees a horse's mane and a crown, and, beyond that, distance, setbacks, courage. Together, they are the sum total of anybody's life.

She discards the leftover coffee in the sink and joins me at the kitchen table. Ever since her husband passed in a car accident, fortune-telling has become her favorite pastime. When Muhsin is away with his other wife, Shirin spends the night with me. We reminisce about the villages of northern Iran bordered by emerald green jungles, about taking remedial science class over the summer, about moving to Tehran and attending the American school. It was there that Shirin discovered she was beautiful and eventually became our nation's first "Miss Persia." We look at her wedding pictures and the unfulfilled promises of love and youth. There were no clues then that her husband, now long dead, had contracted syphilis and wittingly, even vengefully, sought to infect his beautiful bride with it, as if to insure that no other man would ever touch her. "He never told me about it," she admits. "I didn't know to ask. I was only fifteen." Shirin rubs her stomach when she speaks, as if to lament the children she was too afraid to carry in her body.

Martyrdom Street

There is a knock on the door and I walk to the living room to answer it. Three boys, maybe sixteen or seventeen and holding heavy rifles, greet me as I open the door. "I'm with the Komiteh," one of them says to legitimate his intrusion. I'm not sure whether to believe them. They seem nervous, fidgety even, to belong to the Komiteh, the Iranian moral police. By now, Shirin has joined me in the living room. "Put those away," she tells them. "Your guns don't scare us any more."

"We're looking for Muhsin Gilani," one boy says. "Does he live here?"

I wait for him to continue.

"We have to talk to him," the boy insists.

"Who are you?" I ask. "Do you have any papers?"

"We don't need papers," he says. "We've got guns."

"He's at work," Shirin offers.

"What kind of man leaves two women alone at night?" he asks.

"Watch it, son," Shirin cautions. "We're old enough to be your mothers."

The boy in the middle pulls his friend away. "Let's go," he whispers.

"We'll be back," the other one taunts as he steps out.

After they leave, Shirin insists that I call Muhsin. But she knows I don't like to call him at Afsaneh's. I try to convince her that the boys are just harmless pranksters looking for adventure, but she does not relent. The kitchen window faces the street, and even though it's dark, one of the boys peers inside the house as he walks up the road. Maybe somebody really is after Muhsin. After all, he's had brushes with the law before, not for smoking opium but for political talk. Usually his troubles were trivial. He was never a leader of any kind, just a follower. Once or twice, he attended secret meetings at people's homes, typically other professors at the university, to ramble about inequality and the exploitation of the masses, and then to smoke opium as a kind of bonding ritual and grand finale.

After dilly-dallying a bit, I decide to call my brother-in-law. When he recognizes my voice, I tell him what's happened. My brother-in-law remains quiet for a few minutes. Then he orders me to shut off the lights and wait for him at home. Within half an hour, he appears at the house. "Hurry up, hurry up," he urges as I open the door. Muhsin, cloaked in a black chador and full veil, enters first. Muhsin looks ridiculous, and when I see him, I burst out laughing.

"Did you forget you have a moustache?" I say.

Emerald Forests

During the years when our country still cherished its kings, moustaches connoted virility and intelligence. Now they intimate corruption and collusion, and every man I know wears a moustache, including Muhsin.

"Stop it, Fatemeh," my brother-in-law snaps. "You don't look much better yourself."

What? Did I forget to pluck the hairs around my lips again?

His snapping makes me laugh harder. I notice the wart on my brother-in-law's temple as he pushes me away to shut the door. The wart wiggles every time he moves his head, and the light casts shadows, exaggerating the angle where the growth has developed. I laugh more and try not to look at the wart. Muhsin takes off his chador, rolls it into a ball, and throws it in my face.

"Is this better?" he asks.

"Sure," I say, still laughing.

Shirin hands me some ice water. I want to start a sentence, but it's so hard. I can't stop laughing. Wholeheartedly. Consummately. My stomach muscles are cramping up, but I can't stop. There's more laughter in me.

"Here, drink this," Muhsin says, bringing the glass of ice water to my lips.

He forces the water down my throat. But it spills all over my skirt and the Persian carpet, and I laugh even harder. Shirin joins in the laughter as Muhsin gets up to bring some napkins. She understands. The laughter calms my nerves like a lullaby or bedtime story. My brother-in-law wipes the rug vigorously, thrusting his upper body into every stroke. The more frantically he wipes, the more I laugh. I want to ask him to stop, but I choke on my words. Tears start rolling down my face. I hold my stomach and bend over in my seat, staring into his black eyes, still laughing. Muhsin holds me tightly to stop me from shaking in his arms. "Stop it," he pleads, "please, just stop." As I try to return his embrace, I drop in his lap and then my body stops. I hold him, he holds me back and we freeze in that position. "They won't be returning," he whispers. "I promise."

Nasrin

A trail of empty branches hangs at odd angles, extending beyond the boundaries of Central Park. Even the perennials, whose green glistens with the winter frost, tilt their necks like a brigade of defeated soldiers. Only a string of white hyacinths along the bike trail survives the chill. Sometimes strolling in the city reminds me of walking on Martyrdom Street. But Yasaman doesn't seem to notice, picking up the pace and moving fast toward our point of rendezvous.

"Notice how dead everything looks?" I ask.

Yasaman shrugs her shoulders. It's February, and she doesn't expect more. I don't know. The season alone can't account for this inertia. Maybe it's the absence of birds, or lovers, or beggars. Other people sense it, too. Grimacing pedestrians brush past each other, hurrying to reach their next destination. Street vendors, so busy warming their hands, can't bother to attract customers. Nobody smiles. Even the city dogs growl as their owners prod them on.

Yasaman spots a vacant bench near the water fountain and leads us toward it. Nearby, several policemen fiercely guard their "Do Not Cross" barricades, but there are no demonstrators carrying banners or yelling racy slogans, as we expect to find.

"Are you sure we have the right place?"

"I'm sure," Yasaman says.

She unfolds the red flier and points to the print.

"Maybe the rally's been canceled," I say.

"Or maybe nobody decided to show up."

Fereydun appears and taps her on the shoulder as she puts away the flier. He explains that the rally's been moved to Washington Square. Fereydun is running for a political seat in Manhattan.

Yasaman and I exchange curious looks. Then Yasaman goes red and blurts out, "Great. How are people supposed to know?"

Fereydun tells her that they placed an ad in the paper and publicized the change on their Web site. "Most people knew about it," he says.

Yasaman grunts and looks at me. "Obviously, they didn't know about it, either," she continues, pointing to the cops.

Fereydun doesn't advance the conversation. He's used to Yasaman's tantrums. Instead, he fetches a cab and we head toward the Village. There isn't a single tree in sight from there to Washington Square Park.

People of all ages are gathered outside Violetta's Café. A bald man shouts "Down with terrorism" through a loudspeaker and the demonstrators, many of them students, repeat the chant. Within minutes, I recognize the faces of several Iranians I haven't seen in months, even years. There is a former classmate from

Iran, Golnaz, the daughter of the former minister of tourism, who is sporting a designer purse and fur coat that hangs open in the front to expose her expensive outfit underneath. With all the money she spends on clothes, doesn't Golnaz know that you don't wear black miniskirts with opaque beige pantyhose?

Golnaz approaches and we chat briefly.

"I didn't know you were in New York," she comments.

She stares at my outfit, and I suck in my stomach.

"I just moved here a couple of months ago," I say.

"Working?"

"Yeah. You?"

"No. I was just married."

"Really? Hadn't heard," I lie.

She points to a bald man holding leaflets. Except for her hair color, which is now a shiny metallic yellow, Golnaz hasn't changed much over the years. She still obsesses about whose company she keeps, staying friendly with those Iranians who'd robbed and then bought acres and acres of foreign real estate . . . not unlike Golnaz's family. Of course, Golnaz's family hadn't robbed (at least that's what they claimed). But you can never tell with the expatriates. So many have changed names, passports, and wives. It'd be difficult to trace any of their claims here.

I decide to leave Golnaz. She looks a little disappointed that our conversation has abruptly ended but tries not to show it. Fereydun is pleased that a fairly large crowd has turned up for his political campaign. He's an unapologetic monarchist, while Yasaman is still trying to fit in somewhere on the murky spectrum of Iranian politics. Activists on all sides find her too frivolous for their taste, though PERSIA, the Party of Exiled Reformist Supporters of Iran in America— and incidentally, the organizer of today's rally—calls her a nationalist, whatever that means. Fereydun is the president.

As the crowd moves beyond the library, I sit on an empty bench next to the water fountain to read the newspaper. Without warning, a man shoves a microphone in my face and asks, "Are you Iranian, too?" I nod, and he demands to know my opinion on Iran, its president, the economy, and of course, life for women. I'm no expert, I tell him, hoping he will move on to Fereydun or somebody else, but his curiosity deepens. I insist that I don't know what's going on, that there are people far more informed than I, but he doesn't budge. I tell him that I am apolitical, that I don't believe in demonstrations or public spectacles.

"Do you have family there?" he asks. I tell him that my parents still live there but emphasize that they are apolitical, insignificant, and ordinary as well. All of this, though, attracts him more. He wants to know my name, my profession, what I think about the United States. I make up a fake name and profession—"Maryam" and "corporate lawyer"—and tell him how much I like blue jeans and the stock market. He seems satisfied with my response and then asks why I'm not veiled.

Just then, there is a loud sound and a barrage of gunshots. Several protesters run toward the southwest corner of Violetta's Café, where the television cameras, loudspeakers, and banners are placed. My overzealous reporter-friend rushes to the scene and joins the commotion. I wait in the background for some information and direction. Then Yasaman emerges from the crowd, her hair disheveled and her shirt streaked with blood. She is as white as a hospital sheet. I force my way through the demonstrators and hurry toward her. She grabs my arm as soon as she sees me. In between short breaths, she tells me that Fereydun has been shot in the arm. Apparently, it was not an act of political retaliation.

We rush to Fereydun, who is several feet away, propped up next to a tree and being attended by EMS workers. Near him, there are three other men, all of them also wounded but none apparently very seriously. He smiles feebly when he sees us, and Yasaman tells him that the police have already arrested the guy. It turns out he was a local, someone who regularly hangs out in the park. A homeless, a schizo, or something like that, but Fereydun doesn't believe it. He insists the shooting was politically motivated. I try to take his mind off the pain by reminding him that all great political activists pay dearly for their convictions, but that does little to appease him. Still, he manages to sound positive for us. "At least no one can accuse us of organizing another boring rally," he jokes, which is true.

On the way to the hospital, Yasaman, relieved that Fereydun is okay, takes note of all the "important" people she saw at the rally, hoping even more will show up at the Fereydun's fundraising banquet next week. "Did you see him?" Yasaman asks me quietly, so Fereydun can't hear.

I nod.

"He's put on some weight, don't you think?"

A rhetorical question that I choose not to respond to.

"And I think he came alone," she adds.

Taymour and Yasaman used to date briefly, very briefly, say, about a month, and in fact not a lot of people knew about it—a remarkable feat, given the multilayered web of social relationships connecting the exiled Iranians of New York. Yasaman never told me what happened, but apparently he was looking for someone more glamorous, someone with connections to the non-Iranian New York elite, and Yasaman didn't exactly fit the bill. That he showed up today is a bit of surprise, but maybe the possibility of getting in the newspaper proved too appealing to resist.

Aside from the royalist groupies—those descendants claiming a blue-blooded lineage dating back to the Safavid empire—there were representatives of the more recent, and therefore less captivating, deposed Pahlavi dynasty at the rally as well, curiously humble next to their rival royal claimants. Yasaman doesn't take sides in this dynastic rivalry. She's visibly pleased that they all deigned to attend the rally to support this public appeal for the reinstatement of the Iranian monarchy, which would once again enable them to wield power in the country.

"Even some professors showed up," Yasaman continues. "Do you know Dr. Imami?"

I shake my head.

"He's a member of the Council on Foreign Relations," she adds. "Hey Fereydun, don't you think we should invite him and his wife to dinner sometime?"

Fereydun wavers.

"Oh God," Yasaman exclaims, "is he going to faint?"

The attendant doesn't respond but quickly checks Fereydun's blood pressure and injects something into his arm. Within a few minutes, we arrive at the hospital and Fereydun is wheeled into the emergency room while we wait. Repentant for caring more about the rally than about Fereydun, Yasaman walks over to the spruced-up garden outside the hospital entrance and plucks two blossoms from the yellow hyacinths.

An hour passes and eventually we join Fereydun in his hospital room. Yasaman puts the hyacinths in a glass of water on the table near his bed. Fereydun doesn't probe Yasaman's penchant for hyacinths. To him, hyacinths are just flowers. He inhales their innocent aroma and reaches for her hand.

Yasaman

Please don't ask me about the first time we met. I don't remember much except for his gray-streaked beard and long, black lashes. I've never gotten close enough to see how deep the wrinkles are around his eyes. I saw him at a café on Madison Avenue around four o'clock in the afternoon. He was sitting in the corner of a diner, and I watched him in the mirror as he ripped the little white bags of sugar and poured them into his coffee. There was a silent rhythm to his motions, the way his head bobbed back and forth as he stirred his coffee. Then he lifted his cup and noticed me in the mirror.

I met him again at a party. A friend we knew well was celebrating a belated birthday. He was talking to a pale, blond-haired woman next to the bar. Sylvia, Maria, something like that. She was stroking his hands softly, whenever she thought nobody was looking. He blew smoke in her face and she smiled dreamily, blinded by the image of a blissful future. I watched them leave the party together.

Ali sees me often (though I don't think he realizes it) in the café near my house or at the pastry shop across the street. I recognize his black scarf from afar when he walks down Third Avenue. It hangs from his neck like a damp bathroom towel dangling from a hook. It reminds me of the long, somber expression he carries, ambling from block to block. On weekends, he strolls in the park. Forlorn and purposeless. Once I followed him there. I don't think he saw me, but I watched him feed the pigeons and ride around the carousel with a little boy around six or seven years old. Is it possible to connect with a total stranger? That's how it is with Ali. I can't exactly put my finger on it now. Maybe it's something we've both misplaced, like childhood innocence or even something as banal as love.

At seven o'clock he leaves the Fashion Academy. I know because I read it on his syllabus. That's just ten minutes from now. I watch the building from the diner across the street. When I see him, I'll follow him into the subway. He likes bookstores. I lost him once in the Strand. He wove too quickly through the aisles. Maybe tonight he'll go there again.

"Menu?"

I nod.

The tea is cold and tasteless. I ask for a slice of lemon and sweeteners. But they don't help much. This is the sort of tea my mother serves. Bland and colorless. I haven't seen her since last summer. I order a coffee and drink that instead. Small crowds of students form outside the main entrance to the institute. Their tall heads stand out as they move in the streets. I'm thinking about enrolling next semester to study watercolors. I tried painting the other night. The river.

Emerald Forests

The garden. The stop sign. But my paintings lacked magic. I want to rediscover that soft, delicate stroke I had. I can see it in the two or three paintings I've kept: "The Hyacinths," which I painted from the shooting and "Parsa" from when we traveled to Shiraz. The rest are probably somewhere in Iran, rotting away in a stranger's basement.

Oh, wait. On the treeless corner of the sidewalk. I see him now. The black scarf. He is wrapping it tightly around his neck. I leave two quarters and step outside. But he isn't going toward the subway. What's happening? I look the other way. I don't want him to stare directly into my face. He stops at the red light and talks to a young woman. I wait for them on my side of the street, though I pretend to be looking at a window display.

Ali and the woman are talking about some fashion show. I don't know where they are going but I follow them, at least five steps behind. Suddenly, a man with eight dogs appears in front of me. "Excuse me," I say, but he doesn't move. He can't. One of the dogs is defecating. I try to maneuver between the man and his dogs, but we are in the middle of rush hour. People are moving in all directions. When I finally cross the street, I look for Ali's head, but I don't see him. I walk down a side street. Still no sign of him. I enter two cafés, but he's not there either. Nowhere. I can't believe this. I've lost him again.

Fatemeh

At the cemetery, a tulip-shaped fountain spews cherry water in imitation of the blood of martyrs. An old woman wrapped in a black chador fills an empty pickle jar with the red solution. As she shuts the lid, she notices me and takes out a picture from her purse. "My son-in-law," she says. "They made my daughter a widow." Then she walks over to a grave and instead of washing it with the traditional rose water, she pours the red liquid over the tombstone. "I want him to know this is how we remember him."

Just then, two young Komiteh guards approach her, and one of them taps her with his rifle. "This water isn't for you," he says, pointing to the fountain. He stays close behind her.

She gets up, takes the rifle, and points it to his chest. "Now what are you going to do?" She taunts him with her eyes. The guard apologizes and walks away to the opposite corner of the cemetery. The woman throws the pickle jar to the ground and smiles broadly when it breaks into countless bits. This harmless act of civil disobedience seems to give her a moment of peace before she leaves the grounds. Just as well, since right after the woman exits, the fountain sputters and shuts down. This part of the city must be enduring another blackout. For the next few hours this colorful tribute to our war heroes won't function.

The cemetery is located on the south side of Tehran, only fifteen minutes away from the travel bureau. The roads are unusually free of traffic and within ten minutes I reach the passport office. At the door, a government employee, a middle-aged woman, chides a young mother in the unfaltering voice of a believer: "Sister, wipe your makeup off. This is no way to appear in public." She hands the young woman a Kleenex and sends her on her way. Minutes later, another young woman enters the inspection booth and the middle-aged employee asks this lady to take off her shoes. This time, the employee chastises the woman for wearing thin nylons that show her feet in public. "Here," she says, handing her a pair of dirty, opaque wool black socks. "Put this pair on over your nylons." The lady objects but gives in when it becomes obvious that she will not be granted permission to enter the government building and carry on her business with thin socks.

Angered by the harassment, a clean-cut man rises to the young woman's defense: "I can't see her feet," he says. "Just leave her alone." Beads of sweat stream down his cheeks as he growls at the employee, ready to hurl another invective at her. But when a male guard approaches and tells him to quiet down, he backs off.

As I wait in line behind the entrance to the inspection booth, I begin to feel overheated underneath my Islamic robe. I count the bodies ahead of me to see when it will be my turn. But it doesn't come up in time. My head whirls, and I move aside next to a tree to empty my stomach. I must have caused quite a stir because several people walk over to help me. One of them tells me he's a doctor, but his wife yanks his sleeves, wresting him away from the crowd. "Let's go," she says, but the man resists. "Please," his wife continues, "if you touch her, they'll call it fornication and arrest you."

With some effort, I stand in line again. The government employee approaches to see if I want something to drink. When I answer yes, she walks over to the fruit stand across the street. "Orange juice will do you some good," she says, handing me a paper cup. I offer to pay but she refuses my money. She speaks to one of her supervisors, and he quickly looks over my papers. He voids the old passport and returns it to me along with the new one. The old passport has a picture of Nasrin in it, taken long ago. Who knew then that our family would someday be scattered like marbles across wide continents?

Nothing. I hit the radio twice and wait for a sound. The clock is stuck at ten o'clock. Then, without warning, the radio blasts the evening call to prayer. The electricity is back on. As I walk across the living room to put the new passport on the coffee table, I stumble on Muhsin's briefcase. He did not tell me he'd be coming home tonight. Muhsin throws his jacket on a chair, and I watch him take off his shoes before sitting next to me on the couch. We don't speak to each other. He lights a cigarette and the smell of disease spreads through the house. He picks up the passport, flips through it, and tosses it back on the table. Then he walks to the other room to work on the manuscript of his latest engineering textbook. Papers accumulate on the long wooden table in the dining room. He creates neat piles and writes pages and pages in mathematical shorthand. A thick blue vein juts out of his forehead as he leans over his notes. Muhsin looks old.

Thoughts roam in his head. I bring him a cup of tea and some sweets. His hands unselfconsciously record his erratic musings on a yellow paper napkin. When he sees me, he put his notes away, grateful for a distraction. "Thanks," he says, as he covers the napkin he has been drawing on. I push his hands away and see a column of numbers copied over and over again. Although I don't ask, he interprets the numbers for me. "That's how many days I haven't seen her," he says, referring to our daughter, Nasrin. "In a few hours, it'll be 3,678." Then he crumples up the napkin and puts it in the ashtray. For the rest of the night, he stays up completing page after page of his manuscript, until dawn comes and brings with it another day of separation.

Virgin Bride

Nasrin

On the far corner of Broadway, a man takes refuge from the rain under a blue awning. He unfolds a table and slowly arranges his merchandise. Sorting through his umbrellas, he yells, "Five dulla, five dulla, five dulla . . . all sizes, evey culla, five dulla . . ." A young boy, maybe his grandson, stands at his side, guarding the money. The boy leafs through the accumulated dollar bills with a grin. When a passerby suspiciously approaches their stand, the old man shields the boy with his body, showing the same vigilance the demonstrators did when sheltering their children from gunfire on the eve of the revolution.

I stare from the window, half-expecting to be covered again with the blood of zealots. But today there are no rioters in the streets. Only an old man shaking his finger at a boy and speaking to him in what appears to be the language of admonishment. I leave them and walk down a hallway lined with hand-me-down plants. It's been a long week at the Livingston Language Center, a small translating office on lower Broadway. Our company manages international clients, mostly Third World dealers, and I handle the Middle Eastern customers. My official title at work is "Middle East associate." When I show people my business card, they mistake me for a *Nightline* correspondent. → what does that even mean?

We translate everything from Persian to French, to Pashto, to Arabic . . . to any other Middle Eastern dialect one can think of, and of course, to English. They pay us per page, so we work extra hours translating long documents to earn more money: documents about shopping malls under construction, birth certificates, manuals on tubular products (iron, steel, aluminum), instructions for IBM computers, and pamphlets on electronic Mr. Coffee pots. There is a real market for translation these days. Large companies are always looking for ways to sell their gadgets to Third

Virgin Bride

World countries. Sometimes, I feel a little guilty about helping them. When I return to my desk, I finish a typical document—a personal identification form that belongs to an Afghani woman born in 1954, one meter 64 centimeters tall. This translation will be my last one for the day. My eyes are aching from the computer glare, and I stack the translated letters into a neat pile on the desk.

As I leave the building, a woman's raucous laughter seeps out of a nearby bar. I consider stopping at Clarissa's, a Wall Street hangout known for its cheap dark beer, where young, ambitious investment bankers flash their business cards for a date. I already have a collection of them in my purse. Men's and women's, but tonight I don't feel like mingling. On the street, the young boy behind the stand waves a red umbrella at me when I walk by. When I show him my black umbrella, he turns his attention to another potential customer, and I walk on. Rain darkens the air, hastening the approach of night. The future I've been avoiding suddenly feels ominously close.

I let my umbrella drip water into the soiled puddle on the subway platform while I wait for the number 4 train. As I dole out change to a beggar, the train arrives, and I'm happy that I don't have to fight my way for a seat. Rush hours are especially taxing on short people. The subway ride is bumpy, but for once, the train does not stop in the tunnel between Fourteenth and Forty-second Streets. I wonder if Yasaman will be in. My head feels heavy, and I think less about Yasaman and more about sleep. Lately, I haven't been able to sleep very well. I dream short dreams about flying: flying to unknown villages, flying over vast gardens, flying over ancient ruins. But I never seem to have a destination.

Yasaman's shoes aren't scattered across the floor when I enter the apartment, which means she's already left for dinner. Since Yasaman keeps her own hours, it's hard to know her whereabouts. Self-indulgence keeps her busy on an irregular schedule. I glance at my watch and walk over to the bedroom to change. Hamid should be outside the building in five minutes, but I allot an extra ten knowing he'll probably be late. I go to the closet and winnow through my clothes, searching for an outfit that will strike the right balance between blasé and chic. Clothes have a way of capturing a date. I don't want to doom the evening before it begins so I settle for something that he hasn't seen on me before. As I put on my coat, the doorman buzzes me from downstairs.

"I thought we might go to this art show in Soho," Hamid says, as he greets me.

"Okay," I say.

"It shouldn't last long. Maybe we can get dinner afterward."

Then it's time for the usual pleasantries.

"How was your day?" Hamid asks.

"Boring," I say. "Yours?"

"The same."

We hail a cab on the next block now that the formalities are over.

"So what's this art show about?" I ask when we climb into the taxi.

"I'm not exactly sure, but everyone is talking about it. Apparently, the artist is an Iranian lady who paints nude pregnant women with thin veils on their heads."

"No wonder you wanted to go," I say.

"What do you mean?"

"You know."

Hamid acts coy and lowers his head. The cab driver drops us off on Prince Street. We walk down the block, passing the clothing stores and cafés, until we reach a glass door. Several people are queued outside to show their tickets, and we line up behind them. This is, as one might expect, another invitation-only New York City private event. The gallery swims with connoisseurs, art critics, and the occasional casual observer. An older woman in a fitted black leather dress removes her mink jacket to expose bare shoulders. She listens to me make a pointed comment about the insipid use of nudity in French films and then turns to her companion, a young man roughly the same age as me.

"This way," Hamid says, yanking my arm and leading me to a larger room with dim lighting. Several paintings of pregnant women are displayed against the pasty white walls. The first one features a bald woman lying on her back next to a creek. At first glance she looks healthy, but close up, pink blotches discolor her skin. Only the presence of a yellow butterfly hovering above her naked body offers a moment of serenity, a tranquility I find strangely disturbing. The painting is titled *Spring Aborted*.

The next one spotlights a pregnant woman kneeling on the gravel outside the entrance to a mosque. Her face is hidden from view, but she holds a sword in her left hand. Except for a stray autumn leaf, the painting subsists on dusky grayness. The last one situates a pregnant woman and her male companion in a boat. The man fixes his gaze on a handwritten letter, completely unaware of the woman's invitation.

"Well, what do you think?" Hamid asks.

"I need to let it sink in," I say.

"Come on," he insists. "It's only me. You don't need to be so interpretive."

"Okay. The butterfly. The sword. What's the connection?"

"Don't you get it? It's the randomness of everything around them."

"But they seem so deliberately pregnant. Defiantly even."

"Actually, they look needy to me."

"What do you mean?"

"I mean the pregnancy theme itself. It shows that the women are lonely, desperate, and can only turn to their bodies for support. They're in need of constant company."

"No way," I say. "Even the pregnancy leaves them empty and unfulfilled."

"Look, the artist's sitting over there," Hamid says. "Why don't we ask her?"

But as he starts to walk toward her, I hold him back.

"What's the matter?" he asks.

"Don't."

"Why not?"

"I prefer not knowing for sure."

The moon flickers behind dense clouds, hidden from view like a virgin bride. Hamid marches in the streets with his black leather boots, hammering the sidewalk like a judge striking his gavel. He even summons the moon, which displays its face for a moment. As we approach the Citicorp building, his strides grow purposeful. Yet the more assured his gait becomes, the less certain I feel about the evening. What would Hamid say if he knew?

"Is Italian okay?" Hamid asks.

"Sure," I say. "Sounds great."

We head toward the restaurant, which is two blocks away. As the waiter seats us, I quickly survey the room to make sure no one I know is around.

"Are you expecting someone?" he asks.

"Of course not," I say, slightly taken aback.

There's no way Hamid would know. The waitress comes and takes our order. I smile as he talks about his new projects at work. Then Hamid asks if I'm excited about my mother coming in a few weeks for our engagement party and wedding. "Sure," I say. But I haven't seen my mother in years, although we talk regularly on the phone. Then he moves on to more innocuous topics of conversation like the stock market, the weather, and Fereydun's plans to organize the PERSIA banquet.

The squeals of laughing pedestrians invade the apartment. To mute their voices, I place a CD in the stereo and turn the volume to high. Why had things turned out this way? Sometimes, when the apartment is empty, I talk out loud to offer myself reasonable explanations, but I'm tired of the same conversations with myself. Instead, I find a few old photographs and the poetry collection. I don't know what I expect to find, but like a historian I flip through the past, seeking signposts for the future.

Fatemeh

Buildings. Everywhere you look, there are buildings. On Inqilab Avenue, two solitary walls stand on the left side of the road. It's anybody's guess what this pile of rubble will turn out to be. Maybe a mosque, a business center, or a mall. Or better yet, a monument honoring the dead. The drilling sounds fade as I move beyond the construction zone. Ali Agha, the baker, spits out orange seeds on the cracked cement as he counts some change in his hand. Come to think of it, even his store is a new addition to the street.

"What time is it?" Ali Agha asks as he watches the pedestrians on the opposite corner of the sidewalk. A worker tells him the time from inside the bread shop. "It's slow again today," he says, mostly to himself. When he recognizes a customer, Ali Agha motions to his cronies to bring out the sheets of warm lavash. "Hurry up! Hurry up!" he yells, now sitting erect on the edge of his chair. As the man approaches, Ali Agha holds out the bread and says, "Fresh out of the oven. Don't you want to take some home to your wife?" The pedestrian lowers his head, quickly walking away, and Ali Agha curses at a young employee before eating the bread himself. "How am I supposed to run a business?" he complains. "What's their excuse now? The war is finally over."

As I walk past the bread shop, Ali Agha notices me, and the scene repeats itself. "I was waiting for you," he says, rising from his chair. "Some bread, Hajji

Khanum?" I don't fault Ali Agha for his sycophantic ways. He smiles. He calls me "Hajji Khanum." He politely holds out the bread. The economy is hard on everybody these days.

"Six sheets," I say.

When I dispense the change, Ali Agha takes my good hand and kisses it. "God bless you!" he exclaims, following up the blessing with a token prayer, but I quickly pull my hand away. Ali Agha apologizes and I walk away fast. So fast that I don't realize I've walked past the post office. I wipe my good hand against my Islamic robe, rubbing it hard into the cloth until I see a spot of blood. I know then that I've atoned for the sin. It's un-Islamic to touch a man's hand. These are fine points we never learned in religion class. Fine points about nails and skin and hair and water and dirt and cotton and wood.

I pass Ali Agha's bread shop every Tuesday on the way to the downtown post office. Today, I take the long route there: through the bazaar and past Muhsin's engineering building. I haven't been to this part of town since the last explosion. Has it already been a year? That day, I stopped by the bazaar. I wanted an appraiser to price our family antiques. They were for my daughter, Nasrin, and I thought she might someday want them for her home. I asked the merchant if he'd be willing to smuggle them out for a modest bribe, but he just rolled his eyes and sighed. I don't know what I was thinking since, back then, leaving Iran wasn't an imminent possibility, with the war dragging on with no end in sight. But in a state of war, denying reality comes more easily than embracing the truth.

Disappointed, I left the bazaar for the post office. A long line curved outside of the building, but compared to the gasoline queues, this one moved swiftly. As I walked in, the mosque projected the noontime prayer call, the *azan,* which echoed in the neighborhood, and a young woman behind me silently mouthed her prayers. Outside, military planes flew low, circling the neighborhood, and only the azan intruded upon their distant drone. When the prayer call finally ended, the young woman spoke softly to me. "They recruited my youngest son for the war," she said. "He's twelve. Do you have a son?"

I shook my head. Then she whispered, "I don't believe in martyrdom."

Before I could answer, an altercation broke out between two customers standing ahead of us in line. "It's my turn," a bearded middle-aged man yelled as he elbowed a veiled woman half his size to claim a spot in front of the post office clerk.

"What do you mean?" the chadori woman challenged. "I've been waiting for twenty minutes." As she was speaking, the woman adjusted her black veil to hide loose strands of hair. Then she turned to the person behind her to say, "Didn't you see him just walk in the door?" But no one rushed to support her cause. Maybe it was the desperation in her voice, the hypocrisy of her chador, or the weakness of her gender that made her appear guilty. Even though the woman was telling the truth, she sounded less sincere than the man.

Finally, the post office clerk intervened to resolve the issue. "Khanum," he said to the chadori woman, "please cooperate. Let this man finish his business. You'll be next." Before the woman could voice another complaint, there was a loud thump. It was a noise I'd never heard before, as if twenty trucks had crashed into one another. From a distance the red-alert signals, which sounded like truncated ambulance sirens, began to toll. The Iraqis had struck something, but nobody seemed to know what.

Helicopters had joined the military planes to survey the streets. Inside, no one hazarded talking, except for the post office clerks, who shouted orders to file people out of the building. "Over here," a young man yelled, and we formed a line behind him. Another loud crash shook the main lobby, and the concrete beneath our feet began to tremble. The young woman standing behind me again prayed silently as she watched a rat scuttle across the floor. Before the rat reached the western end of the lobby, the tiles trembled, and we flew out of the building.

That's all I remember about that Tuesday afternoon. I'm not even sure if the ground was really shaking after the third blast, or whether my knees were betraying me. I'm not sure. Everything happened quickly, maybe within five minutes.

An old man sits in a wheelchair outside the post office entrance—a spot he's claimed since the war. I place the warm sheets of lavash in his lap and step into the building. He mumbles some incoherent words, and I turn around to acknowledge his disjointed utterances, but I know his memory will only register the incident for a few short minutes. As I wait in line, two teenage boys push ahead of me, but I don't see any point in fighting such aggression. Moralizing won't persuade them to jettison their habits.

Virgin Bride

Since the explosion, I've had a lot of free time on my hands so I create mindless chores for myself. I feed the pigeons. I water my garden. Or I visit the post office. Nowadays, the post office certifies all of our letters and packages. Letters with pictures in them or letters with little substance. Perfunctory letters about the weather or the new ice cream store down the block. My daughter, Nasrin, lives in America, but she probably can't read Farsi any more, so why waste time crafting a masterpiece? Still, I prefer descriptive missives myself. Long, discursive letters about winter nights in cold gardens, but Nasrin rarely writes back. When she makes the effort, it hardly seems worth the trouble. Her last one came three months ago: "Hamid looks like Husni Mubarak. I think it's the nose." Hamid is her fiancé. Then she adds, "Are you still praying, Maman?" I'll keep her letter in my purse until the next one arrives.

When the post office clerk eventually takes care of my business, I step outside and walk a short distance. The man in the wheelchair has rolled himself up a block, and when I approach him, he doesn't recognize me. He reaches out for change, and I place a fifty-toman bill in his lap. At the first green light I catch a bus, and from the window I observe other reconstruction projects across the capital.

The government rebuilt this post office six months ago. A businessman who'd lost a son in the war donated large sums of money to renovate the building. For days, construction hands worked to efface any sanguinary remnant of the explosion, burying broken bones and torn clothing under the ground. Still, despite its clean walls and fragrant household plants, this building isn't so different from the old one. Only scattered ruins in the southern corners of the city linger as icons of the war. A chipped wall, a shattered window, a cripple. Where rocks and gravel once covered the streets, new monuments stand in their places. Outside the main drive leading to the post office, school children gather regularly to water fresh flowers. On that street, Martyrdom Street, where the cypress trees keep perennial watch, only the murmurs of the dead keep their memories alive.

Bloom of Jasmine

Yasaman

The bloom of jasmine. The luster of pearl. The jingle of ivory. The flow of coconut milk. The fall of snowflakes. The innocence of clouds. What is white? Does white feel cooler in the summer? Or more serene? Do whites prefer white sports like skiing? Or tell their children white stories on white winter evenings? On the street, white mingles with brown, yellow, and red, but this brand of human paint does not mix well. I never grasped the true meaning of white. Fereydun entered my life and promised that white did not matter, but he left me once for a white. I don't see him in the airport—this is where he met his white.

My hairdresser, Maurice, calls me olive. Middle Eastern olive as opposed to Mediterranean olive, "which is not so thick and shimmers less in the light." But Maurice is wrong. He is afraid of offending me, and "olive" sounds so chic. I'm too dark for olive, especially on my face and arms, from tanning in the sun. I am brown. Maurice pampers my damaged black hair with hot oil treatments and deep scalp massages, chiding me for having dyed my hair blond so many times. "Why?" he asks, refusing to dye my hair light when I request it. Only charcoal black. Maurice prefers dark hues. He is white.

Imagine white granulated sugar melting in a pot. That's me. A deep caramel brown. My grandmother told me that when I was born, my mother was convinced I did not belong to her. I couldn't. I was too dark. When the hospital refused to take me back, my father came after me. He knew I came from him. He was not white.

Fatemeh

The sky is still black, but morning lies just around the corner. Outside, the trees and crickets hide from view, conspiring to delay the arrival of dawn. I open the bedroom window and listen to their movements. I don't know how Muhsin lives with his other wife—where he sleeps, whether he leaves the window open or shut—but I don't speculate. This is my preferred hour of the day, when the streets are quiet and I can watch Muhsin dream. He doesn't feel me stroke his fingers. From the bedside window, rays of light slowly penetrate the bedroom. I place my prayer rug in the middle of the room and begin the *namaz*. The obligatory prayers are brief, but I linger a few minutes longer.

As I put away my prayer rug, Muhsin wakes up prematurely from his sleep. His forehead is covered in sweat and he throws the blanket off his body.

"It was hot," he says. "I felt like I was on fire."

"The window is open," I say.

"I don't know. I was sweating uncontrollably."

"Where were you?" I ask.

"I'm not too sure. Near the Takht-i Jamshid. Under the rubble."

"It was only a dream," I assure him.

But he remains agitated and confused. The samovar brews slowly in the kitchen. I set the breakfast plates and some lavash on the table. Muhsin joins me shortly with a cigarette in hand. He appears more at ease, no doubt relieved to put the night behind him. Since my accident, his nightmares have become more frequent, but we don't always know what causes them. Muhsin walks over to the kitchen counter to turn up the volume on the radio. When the announcer initiates a litany of doleful Arabic prayers, he reaches for an old newspaper on the kitchen table. "Nobody cares about the news any more. All we hear these days are Arabic prayers. What's the matter with Persian? I bet they're afraid people might actually understand the nonsense they're promoting."

"They're just harmless prayers," I say. "Why make such a fuss?"

I place a cup of tea before him. Muhsin smirks at me but doesn't respond. Instead, he fiddles with the shortwave stations until he locates the BBC. Then he relaxes his forehead and continues eating his breakfast. "Much better," he comments, listening attentively to the news summaries, even though there's nothing especially important going on in the world. When the news hour is over, Muhsin goes into the bedroom to change. He yells to me from there and presses me to finish the cleaning quickly. I pretend not to hear him and sing to myself, louder and louder, until he's forced to repeat himself. He marches back into the kitchen and hovers threateningly over me. Then he moves back slightly and starts drying the dishes. I return to the bedroom to take one final look. The bed is made, and an iron bolt locks the window in place. "Don't worry," Muhsin says. "Everything will be the same when you return." But that is not the point. I'm not sure I want to leave, knowing that anything could transpire in my absence.

The sun pierces through dense clouds. Already, a long trail of outdated cars clogs the expressway. A driver to the left of us thrusts his head out the window to yell obscenities at a wayward pedestrian. Further ahead, two cars stall abruptly, choking on leaded fuel, before chugging along. The car's irregular motion and frequent jerky halts make me dizzy. As I open a window to clear my head, noxious fumes waft inside the automobile, and I feel worse. The air is especially dirty in this part of the city.

"Close the window," Muhsin says, suppressing a cough himself.

The airport appears shortly after we exit the expressway. Its concrete buildings look as unfriendly today as they did ten years ago when we escorted Nasrin here. But these days, there are new slogans on the walls. Muhsin reads some of them out loud: "A veil protects a woman's decency and prevents moral corruption." He lets out a loud, devilish laugh, and continues, "Death to the unveiled. Was that ever in the Qur'an?" he asks.

I don't reply. I know this is not him talking, but the opium that makes him irritable.

"Well," he carries on, "no wonder tourism is suffering. This is no way to greet visitors." Inside the building Muhsin points to the portraits of local leaders on the walls and again laughs to himself, but this time he is careful not to attract attention. We do not speak to each other in the check-in line. When the woman behind the counter returns my passport, Muhsin gives me my handbag and says, "We did the right thing." I hesitate. "Look around," he continues, grimacing at the men and women sprawled on the floor of the airport lobby. "There is filth everywhere. We did the right thing sending her away." I'm not so sure, but I don't engage him, since I'm about to leave. Just then, Muhsin takes my hand and whispers, "Please, tell me. Tell me we did the right thing." I want to respond, but a rush of passengers advances toward us. Though I extend my arm awkwardly to reach Muhsin's hand, the crowd forces me toward the gate and I move ahead before touching him. "Good-bye," I yell, "good-bye," but Muhsin does not react. He has already turned around and walked away.

Nasrin

Two crystal birds assemble an invisible nest on top of the television set. I've often listened for their song but have only heard their silence. The birds entered my home on the eve of my first rendezvous with Hamid. It was a cold night, and when Hamid stepped out of his black BMW, he handed me the box that contained the birds. Hamid was dressed in a fancy solid navy suit and striped tie that I thought I had seen in the Sunday *Times* magazine. At a French restaurant nearby, he ordered steak and frites. I would have preferred a dingy Afghani restaurant on Eighth Avenue, something closer to our roots, but Hamid wanted to make an impression.

Over dinner, Hamid talked mostly, and mostly about his lineage . . . his great uncle's political triumphs, his grandfather's famous lovers. I caressed the birds as he spoke, convinced that by the end of the night my touches would induce sweet melodies, but as the evening wore on, only Hamid's voice resounded in the restaurant, and I, too, fell silent with the birds. I don't think Hamid noticed because sometime later he broached the subject of marriage. When Hamid saw me hesitate, he added, "I'd be happy to talk to your parents." For a day or two, I shared my secret with the birds, unaware that my parents were already privy to it. But that didn't matter. It was time. And Nicholas? He was American. No. They said, everyone said, it was time, time to get married, and Hamid was nice enough, rich enough, man enough. It was time. I was getting old, ugly, undesirable, weak. Old. At twenty-five. I was a woman. It was time.

I lie on the couch and pick up an old issue of the *New Yorker*. After skimming an article about an AIDS patient, I put the magazine back on the marble table and turn on the TV softly, hoping not to disturb Yasaman. After shifting back and forth from the Flintstones to the Muppets, I lower the volume and stare in the distance. The scattered images of my interrupted dreams can never be patched back together. Before long, there are footsteps above Kermit's voice. Yasaman reaches for a bathrobe from the hall closet and joins me in the living room.

"Sorry if I woke you," I say.

"No problem, no problem," she assures me with her thick Persian accent. "We're family, I understand."

We aren't really. Several generations ago an ill-fated marriage linked our families together: my grandfather's uncle married Yasaman's mother's grandmother's sister. What did that make us? Hard to say. At best, distant relatives, but we preferred identifying ourselves as cousins, since that seemingly permanent affiliation sustained our solidarity as friends. In many ways we've shared the same twisted destiny: both under five feet, both prone to gastritis, and both ridiculously superstitious. Only our accents betray how differently we've evolved.

"How about some tea?" I suggest.

"Persian or tea bags?"

"Tea bags. They're quicker."

We place two mugs of water in the microwave and wait for the timer to beep. This is how we start every weekend. Some tea, some small talk, some fortune telling. After tea, we sit in a corner of the room and play with a deck of cards to read our fortunes. We shuffle the cards, and in random order read and reread the arrangements, phrase and rephrase the same questions, until the cards contradict themselves. Then, almost in a state of frenzy, one of us will stop and seek another mindless activity.

"What do we do now?" I ask, placing the cards back in the box. Our fortunes hadn't been all that promising.

"I don't know. Let's call some people."

"Why?" I ask, although I suspect why.

"I don't know." A twinkle flashes in her eye, and an evil smile accompanies it. Somehow she reasons that picking on other people will allow her to forget her aches. "He's not home," she announces after dialing Fereydun's house. "I'll call him at work. Maybe he's working today." Fereydun works for HBO. She opens her purse to search for his number but finds little of value underneath the paper scraps and eye pencil shavings. Then she decides against it. "Do you have anybody to call?" she asks, disappointed.

"Not really," I say.

The temptation to fritter the day away increases as the hazy mist outside thickens, but Yasaman and I promised ourselves to cook an Iranian dish. We both know, from our limited experience, that preparing an Iranian meal is an elaborate affair: it requires enormous pots and pans, many spoonfuls of this and that, and special herbs and spices that can only be found in a corner store on Queens Boulevard. We each put on a pair of jeans and a sweater and saunter toward the subway. After fifteen minutes, when the train finally enters the station, Yasaman lunges ahead to grab seats for us. I stare out the window, and when the graffiti on the subway walls multiply, I realize that we are no longer in Manhattan.

In the rocking cart, an old man nods and smiles as he listens to us converse in a language he does not understand. Yasaman sits next to a young woman holding tightly to her son. I wave to the little boy, who makes incomprehensible mutters in between small burps to acknowledge me. When the woman faces us, Yasaman quickly turns the stone of her sapphire ring toward the inside of her palm to conceal the gem. Then I feel a nudge in my side.

"What?" I ask.

"Didn't you hear me ask you when we'd arrive?"

"No. The train's making too much noise."

I don't think Yasaman believes me. She turns her head the other way.

"It smells," she says.

"I know."

"I'm going to put on some perfume." Yasaman opens her purse wide enough to slip her hand through the opening to retrieve her cologne. She sprays our whole row with a $75 bottle of L'Amour's springtime mist, and the old man sitting next to me rises and switches his seat.

The House of Herbs is located directly across the street from the subway station. A middle-aged Iranian couple and their son jointly run the store. Despite their limited space, they have somehow managed to squeeze in goods from at least a dozen underdeveloped countries. Along the walls, they have laid out large straw baskets filled with seeds: sunflower seeds, watermelon seeds, and pumpkin seeds. Above the seeds, they've built shelves to place canned Bulgarian cheese next to the packaged Indian tamarind. The room retains a distinctive odor that is hard to place, as though the owners left open jars of turmeric and cumin, allowing their scent to mix in with the sweet smell of the rosewater sprinkled along the walls. As we enter the store, I look around to see if I recognize any of the customers. I notice Yasaman turning her head, as well. House of Herbs is usually a good place to run into Iranians we haven't seen in months. "Thank God," Yasaman whispers. "We don't know anyone here."

We're no longer speaking Persian to each other. Persian is our secret language, used only when we find ourselves among people of other nationalities. In the House of Herbs, it's pointless to veil our comments by speaking Persian. Here, we have more privacy speaking in English.

"Okay," I say, handing Yasaman a part of the shopping list. "You take half and I'll take half." To finish the shopping quickly and painlessly, we comb the aisles, gathering the necessary ingredients. After ten minutes, Yasaman meets me at the cash register and insists that it is her turn to pay, which, of course, it is not. Finally, the cashier, exasperated, grabs the twenty-dollar bills out of my hand.

When we reach the apartment, Yasaman and I decide to cook a rice dish with a special walnut-based sauce called fesenjan—my mother's favorite. While Yasaman boils the rice, I prepare the sauce. I put a pound of walnuts and some water in the Cuisinart. The walnuts rattle until the blades mince them so finely that they turn into paste. Then I empty the spread into a large pot and add two spoonfuls of pomegranate sauce to it. "I hope I'm doing this right," I say, as I mix in a spice called golpar. I love its pungent, vinegary smell and take a large whiff of it before sprinkling the golden grains gently in the pot. Yasaman walks over to inspect the pot and I turn on the stove to cook the rice.

"Do you think we'll be back in time for me to go to Au Contraire?" Yasaman asks. Au Contraire is Yasaman's absolutely favorite nightclub. "I've made tentative plans with Valerie," she adds.

"Probably," I say. "Here, come try this," I say, lifting a spoonful of fesenjan for Yasaman to taste. She leans over to sample the sauce.

"Mmmm, it's so good," she says.

I can tell Yasaman is lying. I can hear it in her voice.

"I think it needs some lemon juice, though. Isn't it supposed to be more sour?"

"Okay," I concede. "Pour some in if you'd like."

Yasaman adds two spoonfuls of lemon juice and tastes the sauce again.

"Much better, much better," she comments, pleased with her contribution.

We turn off the stove and enter the living room. Yasaman walks over to the stereo and puts on her Gypsy Kings tape. "I love this music," she says, as she salsas across the living room, Iranian style, curling her hands and waving her hips. We sing along in broken Spanish. Yasaman insists that I should go out with her tonight, even though she knows how uncomfortable I feel around her flashy, rich acquaintances who squander their time and their parents' bilked money in Au Contraire. We have nothing in common. I discuss trends in social theory while they promote their business deals. I mention recent books and they inform me about the new Portuguese hairdresser they've found on Park Avenue. Mine is an arrogance groomed by schooling; theirs is a confidence bred by money.

I decide to take a shower before leaving for the airport. Yasaman has decorated her entire bathroom in blue, practically the same shade of blue as the restrooms in Au Contraire, although I hadn't made the connection until now. Blue shower curtains hang from a blue rod above blue tiles. On the blue soap dish, royal blue soaps clash with the heavenly blue toothpaste and toilet paper. I feel out of place with my large floral-patterned orange and yellow towel. We're running late, so I step out of the shower after a quick rinse. At exactly six o'clock, Hamid buzzes us from the lobby. I step into the living room to find my purse. "Yasaman," I yell, "we're leaving." Yasaman fusses in the bathroom with her eyeliner. "Coming," she yells back. From my purse, I retrieve a gold bracelet and put it on my wrist. An excitement streaked with fear colors my mood as I step outside and prepare to meet my mother.

Crows in a Graveyard

Fatemeh

An old photograph slips out of my purse as I step off the plane. The picture was taken five years ago. As I put it back in my wallet, I worry that I might not recognize Nasrin in the airport. Is that possible? Can a mother not recognize her child? Sometimes, when people ask if I have children, I'm tempted to say "no." Long-distance motherhood doesn't carry the privileges of everyday motherhood. A built-in formality characterizes the relationship of a long-distance mother to her child, from the handshakes to the tone of address. Instead of passing through a natural course, conversations follow a set agenda, working down a familiar list of topics, like in a courtroom. "How are yous" are only meant to extract cursory responses. There is a tacit agreement that secrets too embarrassing to reveal should remain buried. I'm guilty of this myself. Nasrin knows nothing about my accident. Or about Muhsin's other wife.

There are two check-in booths at the airport for incoming passengers: one for "all U.S. citizens," and the other for travelers with F1, F2, or tourist visas. I read the "Welcome" signs in different languages as I walk down the corridors of Kennedy airport but know better than to look for one in Persian. A Frenchman stands in the visa line behind me as we approach customs. "Don't worry," he says, trying to calm my fears. "As long as your passport and visa are valid, they'll let you through."

When we reach the window, the Frenchman lets me go first.

"May I see your passport, please?" the customs officer asks.

I place my passport face down on the counter. The official flips through the pages and then walks away with the passport and my other identification forms.

Minutes later, he returns with a female colleague. "We're going to have to take you back with us," he says. I look at the Frenchman, who appears more and more bewildered by the developments.

"What's the matter?" he asks the officer.

"Nothing, sir, she has a special status," he answers.

I bend over to pick up my bags as the female officer signals me to hurry up. "Will you be okay?" the Frenchman whispers as I start walking away. I nod and follow the officer through the authorized personnel zone. We walk down another corridor and enter a room with foreign passengers. Two or three people look up as we walk up to the counter, but they return quickly to their crossword puzzles or entertainment magazines.

The security woman asks what airline I flew on.

"Air France," I whisper. I don't want to be overheard.

"We need to search your suitcases," she explains.

The security woman marks my documents and leaves the room. I walk over to a row of plastic orange seats and sit down next to a small family. No one speaks except for the bald official behind the counter, his young assistant, and the translator. The passengers respond mostly by nodding their heads. After settling in my seat, I open my oversized black leather handbag to retrieve a piece of chocolate and yesterday's newspaper. To avoid the rustling of pages, I decide to read an article on the front page about a woman whipped by the Komiteh for attending a party where alcohol was served, even though such incidents are hardly newsworthy any more, there having been so many of them in the past.

The official calls my name as I put away my newspaper. I wonder why my turn has come up so quickly. I had heard that delays in the Red Card Room exceeded two hours, but maybe passengers traveling alone are dispensed with more expeditiously. I recognize my passport lying wide open in front of the official as I walk to the counter. The assistant asks for my good hand and dips each finger in the blue ink for fingerprinting. He hesitates slightly when he sees my other hand but does not look up until he has finished imprinting every finger.

"Do you understand me, or do you need a translator?" The official does not smile.

"I understand," I say. The translator returns to his seat.

"What's your name?"

"Fatemeh," I say. "Fatemeh Gilani."

He peruses my documents, never looking at my face. "Why did you come to America?"

"To see my daughter," I say.

"Where's your husband?"

"In Tehran."

"Why isn't he here with you?" he asks.

"He's working. He's an engineer."

"Why is your daughter here?" the officer asks

"To study," I answer, trying to keep it simple.

"Do you have any income or other family in the United States?"

"No," I say. "Just distant relatives."

"How distant?" the official interrupts.

"Distant. Third cousins, fourth cousins."

"And any income?" the young assistant inquires.

"Here are my bank statements," I say, handing over a folder filled with receipts.

"Thank you, ma'am." The assistant takes the file to look over my documents. The official glances over his shoulder to inspect the bank notes and then continues, "So tell me, uh, Mrs. . . . uh, let's see, what was it, Mrs. Guleennni, why do you wanna come to the United States?"

I push the veil away from my face without removing it and answer, "To see my daughter."

"What?" he says, cupping his ear. "I can't hear a word you're saying through that veil."

The young assistant glances at me and lowers his head.

"You know," the official continues, "I need to write down on this piece of paper why we should let you in. But you haven't given me any good reasons yet. . . . I'm still waiting."

"I don't have anything else to say." It's four o'clock in the morning, Tehran time, and I've been traveling for eighteen hours. More than anything, I need to sleep.

"How long do you intend to stay?" the official asks.

"Two months," I say, pointing to the date-issued column.

"I'm going to check her bags," the official tells his assistant as he empties my neatly packed skirts across the floor. He searches everything: shirts, shoes, toiletries. He even holds up my underwear and bras to the light to insure that nothing illicit has entered the country. Beneath the layers of clothing and the lining of my suitcases, the official recovers little of interest, except a bag of pistachios and some Caspian Sea caviar.

"You can't bring food into the country," he says, confiscating the caviar and the nuts.

"Nothing else," he announces as he drops my suitcase to the floor. As I bend down to repack my belongings, the official says, "You're lucky. We weren't going to let you through." Then he returns the passport to me. I flip through the pages until I locate the round authorization seal endorsing my entry into the country—a green ring barely the size of a one-toman coin. With my branded passport in hand, I prepare to leave, marveling that an ink smudge so seemingly insignificant can prove so valuable.

Nasrin

A boy holding a teddy bear momentarily loses his parents in the multitude of trolleys and duty-free bags. A woman with a black veil walks by and receives cold glares as she leaves the arrival building. We sit around and wait for news about my mother. When it's apparent that she's delayed, I use the opportunity to visit the ladies' room. "Do you want to come?" I ask Yasaman. After inspecting herself in her Chanel compact mirror, Yasaman chooses not to accompany me. I follow the red arrows to the restroom and glance at my reflection in the mirror. I make sure that my shirt is tucked in and my braid stands straight. Maman hates my sloppiness in public, since she thinks it reflects poorly on her parenting.

As I approach the east wing of the building, I catch Yasaman gesticulating. "There she is, there she is," she yells into the window, pressing her nose against the glass. When Maman finally sees us, we walk over to help with the bags. "Welcome," I say, lowering my eyes and acting coy, as I'm supposed to do. I don't know to react after the greeting. It'll take a few minutes to get used to having a mother again.

For most of the car ride Maman avoids serious conversation, chattering instead about our relatives, including Yasaman's grandmother, who at ninety-one remains cheery and robust. Maman stares out the window as she speaks, digesting the scenery like a child visiting Disneyland for the first time. Everything seems different from her last visit. More traffic lights have a "Don't Turn on Red" sign next to them. The cars in the streets aren't built as big as they used to be. Americans aren't as fat as she remembers them.

After Hamid drops us off at the apartment, Yasaman opens the door and situates Maman in the living room. I go to the kitchen to warm up the dinner. After freshening up, she reaches for her all-purpose traveling purse. It's time for gifts. Maman unzips the side pockets and winnows through scraps of paper to fish out an agate necklace with Qur'anic inscriptions for Yasaman. She has several gifts for me as well, including some recent pictures from the family.

"Did you repaint the house?" I ask, as I flip through the pile.

"No," Maman says, "don't you remember? It's always been brown."

I look for pictures of my father, but only find one in the stack.

"This," Maman explains, "was taken two weeks ago." In the picture, he's standing before the Municipal Building with a copy of his latest book in hand, *Islamic Engineering.*

"At least he's smiling," Yasaman says, which is true. I can't think of anything else to add.

As Maman puts the photos back in her purse, I notice she has difficulty moving her left hand and keeps a glove on it. When I ask her to remove the glove, she insists on wearing it, explaining that her index finger was burnt while she was taking a casserole out of the oven. Over dinner, Maman and Yasaman exchange the usual repartee about my cooking, but Maman does appreciate the fesenjan. As my mother prepares for bed, she insists on sleeping with her black glove. She says the glove is like a neck brace, except for the hands. That's strange, I think. I've never heard of such a thing, but maybe it's makeshift medicine. I turn off the overhead lights and leave the bedroom.

Yasaman invites me to Au Contraire again as I enter the living room. "Are you sure you don't want to come?" she asks, lining her lips with a pumpkin rust lip pencil. She's careful not to color outside the lines like a child drawing in a coloring book.

"I'm sure," I say.

Yasaman watches her reflection in the kitchen window as I pick up a magazine from the marble table. "Do I look okay?" she asks. She has on a tight camel suede skirt with a silk beige shirt tucked in with a leather belt. Her creamsicle eye shadow matches her skirt perfectly. But she insists that the skirt makes her look fat.

Crows in a Graveyard

"You don't look fat at all," I say.

"You're lying," she insists, modeling in front of the couch.

"You look fine," I repeat.

I try not to sound annoyed, even though I quite obviously am. I wait for the door to slam before picking up a magazine. A deep silence fills the apartment, and I begin reading my magazine. Before long, I finish the cover story and start another, but the magazine doesn't induce sleep. I walk to the window and stare down the long street. From time to time, police sirens swirl upward through the nighttime air. As the police cars drive away, I listen for my mother's breathing, expecting deep, sonorous inhalations, but I hear nothing. The apartment feels no different with my mother here, as if she'd not yet arrived or she were no longer living. A hushed mood hangs in the air, as if by consensus the city has agreed to silence. For an instant, I panic and enter the bedroom to check on my mother. At the sound of her even inhalation, voices from the street regain their timbre and filter through the apartment. Maman's gloved hand lies on top of the comforter, steady and alert. I want to touch it, challenge it, discover what it's hiding, but I know I can't. I'd never seen anyone wear a glove to bed until now. A thick leather glove, black as the crows in a graveyard.

As I watch her, I notice for the first time a small brown mole on my mother's left cheek. In all my life I'd never seen that mole, which looks so familiar to me. There's a small mirror next to Yasaman's lamp, and I glance into it to examine mine. The moles look identical. Same size, same shape, and in the same exact location on our faces. Until now, I never imagined that my mother and I might have anything in common.

The beige walls absorb the faint pink glow reflected by Yasaman's bedside lamp. Except for the glove, all the other objects in the room acquire a pink veneer. Even my mother's face has a slight pink glow. As I stare at her, I wonder what she is dreaming, if we have ever shared the same dreams. I can't tell just by looking at her. Tonight, she dreams without expression.

Yasaman

A well-dressed couple enters the banquet hall. The doorman crosses their names off a list and lets them into Au Contraire. Other guests arrive steadily. "You're early tonight," the coat checker tells me. He smiles and accepts his nightly tip from me. I walk over to a small table with free drinks. Next to me, a tall man retrieves a leather cigarette holder and gold lighter from his inside coat pocket. I recognize the lighter because Fereydun has one exactly like it. Without saying a word, he offers me one of his cigarettes. "No, thanks," I say. "I have my own." When he perceives my indifference, he moves on to a striking brunette and repeats the scene. The music softens and I leave the lounge.

An oil painting hangs in the VIP suite. Quite an ugly picture, actually. The sort you find rotting in the basements of old houses. An inscription under the picture reads, "William N. Macaulay—a hero of the First Boer War." His family must have donated money to renovate this lounge, since the room bears Mr. Macaulay's name. The lounge recalls the decorative arts of Tehran country clubs, whose chambers contained magnificent replicas of the king and queen. But Au Contraire isn't your typical private club. It's very upper class, and people stand outside for hours just to get in, but they rarely do unless they bribe the bouncers. To become a member you have to be introduced by a rich and famous person. Its elitist culture makes it the perfect place for our fund-raising banquet. Fereydun stays in the VIP suite to regale his wealthy friends who, he hopes, will donate money to his political campaign. Most of his acquaintances are Au Contraire regulars.

Au Contraire's clientele consists mostly of rich expatriates who've fled their homelands because of coups, revolutions, or civil wars. Typical clubs in New York aren't nearly as cosmopolitan. The ambience is more chic and sophisticated than other places I've visited in the city. But like other late-night hangouts, it has a dance floor, and after midnight it becomes as much of a pickup joint as any other club in New York. Nasrin doesn't understand why I come here all the time. She even refused to come tonight for the banquet. In fact, she regularly chides me for succumbing to the superficiality around me. "I mean," Nasrin complains, "if each of you donated just one-hundredth of the interest from one of your Swiss bank accounts, you could help solve the homeless problem in New York City." Why do poor people always give rich people unsolicited advice on how they should spend their money?

Here, rich expatriates understand each other's language. They appreciate the hassles of visas and I-20 forms. They understand the sophisticated airs they put on for each other, even though they speak in disjointed English: "Hi, I'm a somebody—my family was famous in such-and-such country—can't you tell from the latest-style Cartier watch or the Bulgari necklace around my neck?" We're privileged and spoiled and don't have to make excuses about it.

Crows in a Graveyard

Everyone gathers in the dining room as Fereydun delivers a short speech. He thanks his guests, who've paid a thousand dollars each to attend the banquet. He passes around a catalog listing their names and promises to represent their interests. But the guests, most of them apolitical, entrepreneurial, and generally ignorant, regard the evening as nothing more than a social occasion to flaunt their wealth and stature among fellow Iranians. They sip their champagnes in celebration of themselves, camouflaging their solipsism with the veneer of philanthropy. And in the end, they open their checkbooks and deliver their promises of support in return for the prospect of publicity and exposure, and even a chance to appear in the Sunday *Times* entertainment section.

As the banquet ends, the older crowd prepares to leave while the younger guests move downstairs to the barroom and dance floor. I walk down a dark wooden hallway clouded with smoke. Valerie, an old friend from college, is sitting at her table nursing a drink and waiting for others to arrive. I approach her from behind and tap her on the shoulder. "Meet anyone interesting?" I ask. She shakes her head. I join her at the table and order a Bellini. I spot Mehrdad, an Au Contraire regular, and try to line him up as my dance partner since Fereydun is busy entertaining his guests.

"Bah, bah," he says, sizing me up. "Can I buy you a drink?"

"I have one. Next time."

"How's your friend?"

"What? I can't hear you."

"How's your friend?" he repeats, his voice a grade louder.

"Valerie?"

"Yeah, I guess. Can't remember her name."

Mehrdad has met Valerie at least a dozen times. Selective forgetfulness, though, is an arrogance he uses on non-Iranians whom he doesn't care to impress. But I know him, and I know that Mehrdad isn't considered as good a catch as some of his other friends, like Fereydun and Hamid, who went to Ivy League universities and are descended from aristocratic families. Unlike Fereydun, Mehrdad can't afford to alienate Iranian women with marriage potential like myself. For a minute, he ignores my comments, ogling a blond instead. "Stop staring," I whisper and watch him blush. Mehrdad recovers quickly and takes a drag off his cigarette.

Mehrdad decides to join some friends in the lounge. Valerie and I grab some empty seats next to the bar. She reaches for her drink and watches the male bartender flirt with a male customer sitting beside her. "Look at them," she whispers to me. "Isn't that disgusting?" Valerie can't stand homosexuals. When she was ten, her father left her mother for a younger man, and she's never forgiven him for that. Valerie looks relieved when the bartender retires from his shift. She pulls up her black nylons, which have gathered into small folds around her ankles.

As I look at the time, someone brushes against my back. I look and it's Ali. He apologizes and then orders a glass of cognac. "Do you come here a lot?" he asks. I shake my head. Then I look down and stir my drink, waiting for him to leave. Instead, he finds an empty chair and sits next to me. "What do you do?" he asks.

I tell him that I own a retail clothing store for women, and even though I know where he works, I ask him about his job. As I speak, Ali looks into my eyes, and I feel fat. Is my face shining again? Good thing it's dark in here. I knew I should've worn my hair up tonight. Fereydun always tells me I look prettier that way.

"Would you excuse me for a minute?" I walk past the dance floor to go to the ladies' room. Mehrdad is flirting with the woman he's been eyeing all night. Next to him, there's a classmate from Iran. She's put on some weight since college. Rumor has it that she moved from LA to New York last month to search for a respectable Iranian man. The husband market in LA was bearish, so her family sent her to New York and boosted her market value by buying her an apartment on Park Avenue. She waves to me but I pretend not to notice. As I straighten my hair in the mirror, it occurs to me that I might be making a big mistake trying to befriend Ali. He is divorced. He is older. He has a child. What am I thinking?

Random people drift in and out of the VIP lounge. Ali discusses his work at the Fashion Institute—his latest projects, last month's show in Milan. He invites me to audit one of his classes there. I politely tell him I'll consider it. Drunken voices continue to fill the lounge. The busiest hours here are between 11:00 P.M. and two o'clock in the morning, but the later crowd consists mostly of people my age. Ali looks restless and glances at his watch. "Do you want to go for a walk?" he asks and I nod. Before leaving, I slip upstairs and tell Fereydun that I am going home. He apologizes for not accompanying me and promises to call in the morning.

We walk down the street for a few blocks, past the famous maisons, the Yves Saint Laurents and the Diors, and discuss the latest fashions. Ali's voice sounds serious and intense, but once we walk past the boutiques on Madison Avenue, he drops the subject. "It's getting late," I say, noticing a large digital clock on one of the skyscrapers. Ali understands and stretches out his arm to hail a cab. As the driver pulls over to the curb, Ali removes a crumbled piece of paper from his right pocket and scribbles something down. "Here," he says, folding the paper and handing it to me. "Don't forget next week at Mallery's," he adds just before shutting the door.

The cab ride is short and swift. The taxi driver speeds through five green lights, two yellows, and a red. Within five minutes, we're at the entrance to our building. I quietly open the door and sit alone in the living room for awhile. Then I go to the hall closet and find my drawing pad. At first, I draw stray lines and curves, but soon they begin to take shape. I sketch different versions of the painting I saw in the VIP lounge. There's one of him in a leather jacket; one of him in a fancy suit. For fun, I even draw him with a white turban, but with each new sketch, the portraits resemble Ali more and more. I remove his note from my bag and read it: "Tuesdays and Thursdays, 11:30–12:45—come by whenever you have time." I wonder how Ali runs his classes, whether he's hands-on or standoffish and austere. I paste his note underneath the last portrait in my sketchbook—a drawing of Ali adjusting the folds of a mannequin's skirt.

Crescent Moon

Fatemeh

So. This is how she lives. The apartment looms over Seventy-seventh Street, a concrete high rise with dark windows that shine from the outside. It warns the world to keep away, like a sign reading "Beware of Dogs!" or "Enter at Your Own Risk!" I stare at my reflection in the bedroom mirror. The sight of naked bodies embarrassed me before my marriage. It grew worse when I was pregnant with my first child. Male doctors kept examining with objects I'd never seen before. Even with all their equipment, they couldn't save the child who suffocated in my stomach during the fifth month. Today, my stomach is a lean, flat surface of skin. It hides any signs of the children borne in the womb, repudiating my motherhood. Children inhabit your body—breathe the same air, digest the same food—then grow up as complete strangers. In a new home. In a new country.

There are no photographs here, except for a small silver frame containing a black-and-white snapshot of Yasaman's father when he was a young man. He is standing among the cherry trees in the vast gardens of their family estate. He displays the smile of a man alerting the world that he'll be going places in his life. To a large office building. To the king's palace. To other continents.

It was on that same spot—among the grapevines and the cherry trees—two neighborhood kids barged into the garden and found him playing in the garden with Yasaman and Nasrin. The boys wanted to declare the victory of the revolution. One of them fired three celebratory shots, only he wasn't aiming at the sky. He just cried, "Allah Akbar, Khomeini Rahbar" and shot Yasaman's father once in the head and twice in the heart. His friend stayed longer to say, "Sister, don't cry. Come join the Party of God."

The contorted body rotted slowly as we looked on. Yasaman hovered nearby, watering the hyacinths and singing lullabies. From time to time she touched his bloodied heart and rocked his sun-burned head in her arms. When I told her to go inside she screamed—loud, deafening screams—and then took my hand and placed it on Reza's heart.

"Do you hear?" she asked.

I shook my head.

"Green canaries."

She hummed a melody.

"He's singing with them. Listen."

When I asked what he was singing, she screamed again until she lost her voice and remained silent for the rest of the night. She never talked much about it after that. She was ten.

Tonight, I feel him come out of her silence. He knows I'm here, in his daughter's home, and he watches. I don't know what he wants from me, but that doesn't seem to matter as much as his mere presence. In all my time in Iran after his death, I never once sensed his proximity as I do tonight in this small room that he never saw. It's that lone picture of him that has once again brought him to life.

Nasrin

The cold wind jars the "No Parking" sign on the corner of Seventy-seventh Street. Maman tightens her scarf to keep out the frost. I show her where the bank and post office are located, so that in my absence she can tend to her daily tasks without losing her way in, what seem to her, the labyrinthine streets of New York City. I identify markers to help her remember the way home: a children's shoe store to the right of the post office, a McDonald's across the street from the bank. "I know, I know," Maman cuts me off.

We enter Bloomingdale's from the men's store, zigzagging through the accessories aisles and dodging the perfume models along the way. "We have a free gift today with any purchase of Renée Hauser," a salesman interrupts as we walk toward the escalators. The salesman lets her winnow through the articles in his straw basket. Maman revels in this haven of variety, eagerly lifting the caps off the lipsticks and comparing the different shades of red. There are probably more lipsticks here than there are food items in some grocery stores in Iran. As a customer makes a selection and hands over her credit card, my mother gently tugs at my sleeves. "No haggling?" she whispers. I shake my head. "He's probably ripping her off," Maman concludes. Probably, I think, but that's the point.

We walk to the front of the store to catch the escalator up to the third floor. We follow a sales assistant to the other side of the store, where the outfits are discounted. When we finish picking out an assortment of appropriate gowns for the engagement party, we head toward the dressing rooms. I manage to find a couple of dresses myself, which I hide underneath the pile. Maman flips through each dress, feeling the material and putting the hanger against my back to picture the dress's fit on my body. My favorite is a simple black wool dress I found in the nameless, "clearance sale" collection. It looks comfortable, so I decide to try it on first.

Standing nearly naked under the store's sterile fluorescent lights, with my mother in one corner and the sales assistant in the other, overwhelms me with the same feeling of claustrophobia that pervaded my childhood years. Suddenly I am reliving the incessant put-it-ons and take-it-offs, zip-it-ups and zip-it-downs, tie-it-heres and tie-it-theres. To make matters worse, Maman stares directly at my body, taking note of all the changes that adolescence and adulthood have set in.

"Too tight," I decide and pick another dress from the pile. This one is gray-blue, the color of the Caspian Sea on a breezy autumn afternoon. Although the dress doesn't trumpet festivity, we agree to buy it. The subdued tone of the dress conceals, and for a moment I contemplate confronting Maman about the wedding. But she seems so happy organizing our affairs and again I let the matter slip.

We stop in a deli on our way home and grab some lunch. As I watch the people walk by, I wonder how my mother spends her days in Tehran. She probably walks alone in the streets. Is there anywhere to go other than restaurants? The city has some sports facilities or movie theaters. Other than wedding receptions and religious ceremonies, there aren't too many other forms of entertainment. Maybe my mother spends most of her time visiting relatives. But what then?

What is there to do when all the relatives have been contacted? I try to imagine her sauntering along the roads, but the city's geography eludes me. The streets no longer connect in my head. I see random paths with no destinations.

A turquoise chador drapes Maman's curved back, illuminated from the sunlight like the tiles of the Gawharshad Mosque. There are no changes in the way my mother prays. Her voice still crescendos as she ends the first verse of her prayer. She bows in humility, thankful for so many things. She does not notice me watching her. I try to understand her faith but can't.

Maman folds the prayer rug and puts it on the chest of drawers. Then she walks to the Persian end of the bookshelf to look for something interesting to read. After making her selection, she carries the book to the kitchen and places it on the counter. With her back to me, Maman removes her glove and skims the book to find a familiar passage. Her voice lilts as she recites a scene from the Book of Kings. Rostam, Iran's peerless hero, thrusts the dagger into the enemy, Sohrab, and only then do Rostam's eyes fall upon the charm marking Sohrab's paternity. But it's too late. Persia's valiant warrior has slain his only son.

"Do you remember this story?" she asks.

"Yes," I say. "I never liked it."

"Why?"

"I don't know. Too much pathos."

"What's that? Something bad?"

"Kind of. Just means too many emotions."

I find my copy of the Shahnameh in translation and walk into the kitchen to read along with my mother. I hold the book firmly, eager for our literary exchange. At first, Maman doesn't hear me. She sings to herself. Jumbled phrases, some of which come from a folk song called "The Land of Gilan." Then, when she acknowledges my presence, she stops. She looks for her black glove, which lies on the counter out of her reach. "The plates," she says quickly, throwing a towel on her hand and pretending to dry the dishes. But it's too late. I'm on to her secret now. I've seen the four-fingered hand. Maman carries on as if I'm not in the room. Instead, she lets the water gush out into the sink while humming her Persian folk song.

"How?" I ask.

She doesn't answer. She continues to sing off-key. I close the book and take her wounded hand in mine. Maman tries to pull her hand away, but I hold on. Above the third finger, the knucklebone protrudes unnaturally, causing the pinkie to curl slightly like the tip of a ram's horn. Close up, I notice that there is more than one scar on her hand. In fact, I find a constellation of them, but the one shaped like a crescent moon catches my eye. The moon is imprinted into her flesh above the missing fourth finger.

Unexpectedly, my mother recounts her accident in a string of staccato bursts. The time. The location. The sheer randomness of the attack. Though her words are short and simple, I have difficulty understanding them, and my mind only registers one thought: that the accident would never have happened were it not for the revolution. I'm sure of it. Then Maman stops just as abruptly as she began. Though I feel compelled to speak, I say nothing. I watch my mother, who stares out the kitchen window, somewhere far away, beyond the concrete walls and the barren trees. Two tears trickle onto her hand. Under the fluorescent glow of the kitchen light they illuminate the crescent moon, flickering like distant planets lost in the sky. When she shifts her body, the tear drops slide through the empty crack between her fingers, forever extinguished.

Yasaman

Not in the restaurant. Please go away. Just for a few hours. Don't start that. Why can't you let me be? Soon enough. No. I can't. I'm not listening any more.

"Did you hear me?" Fereydun asks. I apologize and say "no," blaming my inattention on the loud fire trucks outside. I chew on my bread stick and pretend that nothing is out of the ordinary, although I register the scenery as garbled images in my head, like a Salvador Dali painting. Fereydun repeats his question. "Sure," I answer, "we can walk to my boutique after I finish my tea."

Nobody would understand if I tried to explain. I'm not even sure if I understand them. He comes to me every few weeks. Sometimes, in the day. Other times, in my sleep. I heard him for the first time in the basement of my junior high school, on Martyrdom Street, where I was learning how to smoke cigarettes. Suddenly, my ears filled with a dove's moans, and I stopped. At the time, I thought nothing of it. But the whispers resumed. I started hearing him on the Walkman, the television set, or any other electric object that transmitted sound. Once or twice, he tried to make me laugh by imitating others.

"Ready?" Fereydun asks.

"Yeah," I say, gulping down the last sip of my tea.

I'm more relaxed now that he's gone. I can concentrate on Fereydun again. I don't remember what he was talking about, but that doesn't seem to matter. "I'll get this," he offers. He digs into his left pocket looking for change. I watch Fereydun's limber strides as he carries the bill to the counter. Fereydun is tall for an Iranian man. Just around six feet. I hadn't noticed his height until now. Without my heels, we might look asymmetrical, like a shirt with two different sleeve lengths. I'm just under five feet.

Outside, shadows leave mottled specks of gray on the sidewalk. Down the block, a ray of light pierces through the narrow slit between two adjacent buildings. Fereydun walks confidently toward Fifth Avenue. He turns his head from time to time to insure that I haven't fallen behind. "Okay?" he asks and I nod. When we reach the boutique, there are several customers browsing through the dresses and silk blouses. Business usually picks up after five, when the working population once again reclaims the streets of New York City.

Do you remember when I took you to the circus?

Fereydun asks me practical questions about the boutique. Boring questions about the conditions of the lease or the security system I decided to install. He's a lawyer and wants to make sure that the business aspects of my work are taken care of. I've only owned this store for two years. Fereydun looked over all my papers and even tried to convince me to move my boutique to Soho, but I insisted on the East Side because I wanted to be close to my favorite designers. In fact, that's how we met. I needed a good lawyer, and several people gave me his name.

The elephants. You wanted to ride Ali Baba's elephant.

We walk to the evening wear section. Fereydun looks at the labels and price tags and gives me a few tips. Then he asks why I don't market my own designs. "I don't know," I say. "Probably because I'll lose money." He laughs and promises to support me when he wins his next big case. Before leaving, I go over the invoices with Claudia, my manager, and flip through the mail. On a fluorescent green sheet, there's an advertisement about a student fashion show at the

Institute where Ali teaches: "11:00 A.M. March 1st—Klein Auditorium. Free and Open to the Public." Claudia comes to the cashier to ring up a purchase. The shopper is a teenage girl with braces and streaked pink hair. She smiles broadly as Claudia hands her the brown paper bag containing the jacket she has bought. Fereydun and I follow the girl out the door. "I bet you liked shopping without your mother, too," he says with a grin. I nod. My mother and I don't have the same taste in fashion.

The afternoon light fades into dense layers of dark blue space. Cracks and crevices blend into the pavement, no longer visibly obtrusive. As we prepare to cross Fifty-second Street, a car approaches and Fereydun grabs my hand to pull me back toward him. "Watch it," he yells. I tell him that I had no intention of stepping in front of the car, but he remains perturbed by the near accident. Fereydun can't help himself. He overcompensates for everything ever since I discovered his affair with the white woman.

The monkeys threw peanuts at us.

The ringing in my ears grows louder and louder. Though I try to ignore it, nothing works. Not the screeching cars or the sound of my voice. I don't want Fereydun to notice that there's anything wrong, so I carry on with our conversation, even though I have difficulty concentrating. A dog sniffs Fereydun's shoes as we enter his apartment building. Fereydun pats the dog, a golden terrier that reluctantly moves on when prodded by its owner.

Do you remember?

"Something to drink?" Fereydun asks. "Orange juice? Tea?"

"Nothing," I say.

Scraps of paper are scattered before us on the round wooden table. Bills. Subscription notices. Blue aerogram letters written in a child's large, uneven print.

Fereydun brushes aside the paper to look for his pack of Camels. When he finds them underneath the aerogram letters, he offers me one as he lights his own. "Yes, I'd love one," I say, reaching over. Though the room is quiet, the vibrations in my ears resound loudly. I hear distorted voices, spoken as if through a blanket.

Do you remember?

"I remember . . ." I say.

"What?" Fereydun asks.

"Nothing," I say. I remember.

Crescent Moon

Fatemeh

What is it about the air of guilt—the self-conscious twitches, the wandering eyes, and the cautious humor—that invariably gives the guilty away?

With Muhsin, it was the smell of his cigarettes. They no longer released the crisp aroma of fine tobacco. This was the smell of infirmity, the stench of tobacco grown on diseased lands. Maybe Iraqi shelling had damaged the yearly crop, transferring rare viruses from decaying human flesh onto idle land. Or maybe poor manufacturing had stained the tobacco leaves with unwelcome impurities. Pesticides. Fossil fuels. Chemical gas. Whenever Muhsin lit a cigarette, a grayish smoke stretched out sideways, like a sick cat, mutating mild coughs into wild paroxysms.

On that sunny afternoon when the post office exploded, Muhsin had planned to spend the day working at his engineering firm. This line of work had irregular hours. Sometimes during the week Muhsin would be gone all morning; other times he wouldn't even leave the house. I watched him step outside with his cigarettes and fake leather briefcase.

When the bombing threw me onto the concrete, I lay still, thinking of Muhsin. Random scenes passed before my eyes, and I could feel his presence. We were both downtown, maybe just a few streets away from each other. On a map of Tehran, the distance between us measured less than the span between two fingers. I wondered whether Muhsin could hear me if I called out his name. Once or twice, I opened my mouth, but there was nothing. Tall flames spilled out of the sky, and I had difficulty focusing. I was slipping out of consciousness.

During my subsequent phase of alertness I smelled death. A young man lay beside me, heaving with prodigious effort, until he decided, quite abruptly, that life was no longer worth it. That was when I became aware of him—of his putrefied limb and gory perspiration. Dismembered from the rest of him, the man's hand had landed next to my feet. His was a beautiful hand with long artistic fingers and unmanicured nails, a hand capable of painting masterpieces or composing epics. He saw me admire his detached appendage and smiled vaguely. Just at that second, before he decided to surrender his body, his eyes caught mine. They seemed to tell me, "Take it, if that's what you want. It belongs to you now." I've often wondered about him and that hand.

A rescue worker draped a white sheet over his corpse and severed parts when the young man shut his eyes. I shifted slightly as the rescuer's shoes brushed against my side. Then the rescuer placed two fingers on my throat and yelled to his fellow workers, "This one's alive." Two helpers crossed the street and rushed to lift my body onto a wooden stretcher. "Does it hurt?" one of them asked, as he placed me inside the ambulance. It was his question that reminded me of the sensation I'd lost in my left hand. A female attendant nurse rubbed an acrid liquid under my nose as the engine started. "Breathe," she said, gently caressing my face. When my inhalations grew regular, the woman raised my head to cover it with a veil. As she fastened the ends of the black fabric into a loose knot, she pledged, "Have faith, Sister. We'll win the war," but her assistant just bandaged my hand and sneered. What did faith have to do with war?

Someone tried calling Muhsin at the office when we reached the hospital. Nothing major, they had claimed, which was true—just a deep wound in my left hand. As the doctor explained, though the hand was never going to move well, in fact hardly move at all, it was still there, almost in full, attached to the rest of me: "All four fingers and nails," he affirmed, as if there were nothing unusual about the number. He wrapped the gauze tightly around my hand as I watched the lifeless burden on the left side of my body.

Eventually, the nurse wheeled me into another room, away from the other victims of the explosion. She asked again if there was anyone else I wanted to call. "My husband," I repeated. Within minutes she returned to tell me that Muhsin still wasn't around. I suspected nothing. I knew he'd come to me in time. I thought about my hand, about life with one functional hand instead of two. How much could that change a person's life? I could still dust, chop, caress. And Nasrin. How would she take it? It didn't matter then. I wouldn't be seeing her for some time.

Muhsin finally appeared and entered my hospital room without knocking. "Why did you go *there?*" he demanded in an accusatory tone, as though going to the post office carried the same implications as marching onto a battlefield. I didn't answer. The nurse had given me an injection, and my head grew heavy with oblivion. I don't remember him leaving for the night. He returned the next day just as the nurse was changing the dressing on my wounds. He looked away as he spoke, focusing on the door instead of my hand. Evidently, the explosion had started a massive migration out of Tehran. Muhsin rolled in a television set into my room after the nurse finished bandaging my hand. The main station aired several scenes from the explosion. I looked for glimpses of the young man lying beside me, but the reporter had moved on to another newsworthy event: a Tunisian caravan gone astray on the road to Damascus.

"You hear that?" I asked Muhsin. He looked pale. He slipped his fingers through his greasy hair. As he spoke to me, Muhsin caressed my good hand, even though public displays of affection—even between married couples—were against the Islamic rules of the state-run hospital. I wanted him to stop but said nothing. Then, in one ugly second, I began to yank his hand, hoping to pull it out of socket as if it were an appendage on a doll. I yanked and yanked until Muhsin eventually shook me hard and told me to stop. Then he lit a cigarette and the smell of infirmity suffused the room. His eyes drifted away from my face and onto the white tiles beneath his feet.

"I was at work," he said quickly. "On site. It was Tuesday, remember?"

"Nasrin used to count tiles," I said.

"I came as soon as I heard."

"She must have learned that from you."

As Muhsin reached for the pitcher to pour some water, his hands quivered and he spilled the water on the floor. The second time he tried, the glass slipped out of his hands. Never before had an incident so alienated us. Not the revolution, the drugs, or even Muhsin's short stays in prison, I guess, because none seemed as indelible as this. The knowledge of something good turned putrid bothered us, and my crippled hand displayed publicly the imperfection of our lives.

I knew then.

"Why you?" he whispered.

I felt him grope for my anger, but there was nothing. One who has lain next to death begins to hold onto life, however feebly. "It's still in my purse," I told him.

"What?"

"The letter."

"I'll mail it tomorrow," he offered, "and give some money to the poor."

"Please." I pleaded. "Please take care of it."

"I will," he promised.

He never did.

I returned to the hospital weeks later to have the bandages removed from my hand. This time, Muhsin accompanied me throughout the ordeal, valiantly, as if instructed beforehand by the doctor. He did not even cringe when he saw for the first time my twisted fingers and bent knuckles. I did. I wanted to rip my hand away, like a chicken bone, and dump its remnants into a garbage bin—permanently out of sight.

"Try massaging it several times a day," the doctor said. "Soon you'll gain some feeling back." He began rubbing my hand with soft vertical strokes and waited for me to take over. When he released my hand, I let it drop to my side. Instead, from his office window, I watched a stray cat limp to the other side of the street. The doctor paused. "Like this," he offered again, taking my hand and exerting pressure upon it. He waited for me to imitate his motions, but without his encouragement the hand again dropped to my side.

On the way out, the doctor gave Muhsin a bagful of color-coded tubes. "This one numbs the pain; this one will heal the remaining cuts with minimal scarring; this one will . . ." I stopped listening to him, focusing only on the doctor's fourth finger. Would he have responded to his own pain in the same way as he reacted to the suffering of others?

At the first red light, Muhsin kissed my hand ever so gently from the fingertips to the center of the palm. "This point here looks like a bird's nest," he said, referring to the corner where the life line and love line intersect. To me, the indentation looked more like a ditch. As he stroked my arm, his eyes wandered from the wound to the window. I longed to stare at him, into his eyes, but Muhsin twitched as the light turned green, and his eyes followed the afternoon traffic to the other end of town, away from my sight.

Nasrin

A beggar stretches out her hands for change, but the building super sweeps her aside to another corner of the sidewalk. "You're blocking the entrance," the doorman berates a middle-aged bag lady who's laid out her cardboard home in front of our building. Instead, he makes room for a chauffeur to open the door of a white limousine. Maman shakes her head and mumbles something about how disgraceful it is that a country as rich as America has so many suffering poor people. "You never see anything like this in Tehran," she comments. "Never."

We hail a cab and arrive at the restaurant. A waitress leads us to a table in the back of the room. A dark red curtain, the color of dirty blood, drapes the window next to which we're seated. As the waitress lights the burgundy candles that match the curtain, Hamid enters the restaurant. He shakes my mother's hand and apologizes profusely for being late, even though he's on time. "Why don't you sit here?" Maman suggests. She moves over to make room for Hamid next to me. This is our first gathering since the announcement of our engagement, and Maman and Hamid both seem eager to please.

"Did you have a safe trip?" Hamid asks. Maman laughs shyly, confessing how much she hates to fly. I can tell she's pleased with Hamid. She allows him to lead the conversation, preferring to listen instead of talking herself. When the waitress approaches our table, Hamid orders a bottle of wine and stares into my eyes with a gleeful smile on his face.

"What's the matter?" I ask.

"It looks like we're going to move to Dallas," he blurts out.

"Dallas?" I say. I don't know what he's talking about.

"IBM wants to start a major project at their Dallas office."

"Is that what your big meeting was all about today?" I ask.

"That was it. They want me to head it. It's a big promotion."

Though everyone's expecting me to continue, I have nothing to say. I wait for someone else's voice to fill the void. "That's terrific," Maman offers in a high-pitched tone. "You must be excited." She spills some water on the tablecloth as she attempts to initiate a toast. I look around the restaurant to insure that no one is overhearing our conversation. Dallas. Objectively, there's nothing wrong with Dallas. It'd be nice to live in a large house, for a change, and to be in a climate where sun is more the norm than the exception. Dallas can be fun and exciting.

"Dallas?" I repeat quietly.

"Have you ever been there? It's wonderful. We can buy a big house with a garden, where the kids will be able to play as much as they like. New York is no place to raise a family."

"I suppose this won't be for another six months or so," I say.

"Well," Hamid continues with the same sly look in his eyes, "my company's expanding. I told my partners that I'd be married in two months and that we'd be ready to move after that." He reaches for his bag and pulls out a score of gaudy tourist brochures. Underneath the table he rubs his leg against my thigh. I flip through the brochures, staring at the dreamy portraits of Dallas denizens, but all I see is an arid, urban desert. Who'd willingly move there?

Martyrdom Street

Over dinner, we try not to discuss Dallas. We talk about the food, recent movies, and the Iranian community in New York. Hamid asks my mother about the political situation in Tehran, but Maman is careful not to sound too despondent. "You hear exaggerated stories in America," she says, measuring her words. "Things aren't so bad anymore. Most people lead normal lives, now that the war is over."

The restaurant whirs with wholesome chatter. New couples arrive, peopling the booths next to the windows. A man and woman, intoxicated with alcohol, gaze into each other's half-open eyes with everlasting love. When the waitress brings the dessert menus, I emphasize how full and tired I am to encourage Hamid to leave. "Tomorrow is going to be a long day," I say, even though I know tomorrow will be no different from today.

When the waitress finally brings the check, Hamid slips his gold credit card under the bill. We get up to leave, and the waitress calls after us to say, "Don't forget these," handing Hamid the Dallas brochures. He knows not to burden me with them. On the street, Hamid and I don't speak much. Maman decides to try Hamid's car phone. She's amused by his expensive high-tech contraptions. "Sure," he answers, agreeably, handing her the phone. When we reach the apartment, I am the first person out of the car. Maman stays behind a minute longer to invite Hamid in for a cup of tea. "I'd like to," Hamid says, "but I have a meeting early tomorrow morning." Meetings provide Hamid with a convenient excuse to avoid encumbering social obligations. Then turning to me, he asks, "Will you stay for a second? I want to talk to you."

We're alone in the car. "You look beautiful," he says, to mollify my mood I think. I don't respond, even though he looks beautiful, too, with the dim streetlight casting shadows across his cheeks. There's a dreamy glint in his large brown eyes, and I mistake the fatigue for guilt. "You won't hate Dallas," Hamid insists. He takes me into his arms, and I don't resist. I'll have to grow accustomed to his presence.

Yasaman

Ali sketches the outlines of a thin model. His hands move purposefully, unlike mine, without any second thoughts about shape or size. On the next page, he designs three shirts without heads or bodies, filling them in lightly with colored pencils. "The legs you drew are disproportionate to your model's torso. Pare down her calves," he explains, erasing my curves and drawing slick new ones in their place. I watch him shade the drawing as he reconfigures the model's body. "There," he says, cutting out the shirts and placing them on her chest. "Now they fit." I look on, admiring the way he has rescued my pattern. With him, drawing comes effortlessly, like talking. With me, the moves are laborious. I fret over every line, every angle, every curve, every color, and still the final product somehow appears incomplete—imperfect. Ali simply lifts a pencil and allows his fingers to follow their instinct. He does not have to dictate an idea.

We are in his studio working on my portfolio. "I'm glad you decided to stop by," he says. The Fashion Academy is organizing a student fashion show in which Ali has convinced me to participate. "On Monday," he says, "we'll go down to Seventh Avenue and buy the fabrics. I know most of the merchants downtown, and they'll show us everything they have in stock." He watches as I take out the samples of cloth from my bag. Ali takes the drawing pad from my hands and rips out the design he remodeled. Then he finds a thumbtack on his desk and pins the picture above the couch. "This is you," he says. "It was your legs I had in mind," he adds with a smile, and I can feel myself blush, so I change the subject.

"Do you ever draw other things? Or paint?" I ask.

"Sometimes, but lately I haven't done much of anything."

"How about titling your work?"

"Never. I don't like to trap them in time."

It's been three weeks since we started seeing each other. We meet clandestinely at obscure locations in town to avoid the upscale Iranian clientele that frequents nightclubs and uptown restaurants.

"I think you'll win," he says. He kisses my eyelids.

"Really?"

"You're better than my students."

When Ali sits down on the couch, I rest my back against his side, browsing through an old edition of *Women's Wear Weekly*. When Ali is done reviewing—and repairing—my designs, he closes the notebook and begins to rub my back. I find my ad on page 8 and poke Ali to make sure he is aware of it. "Finally, they got my address right," I say, and he laughs. The newspaper had already bungled three ads I had placed for the boutique, but at least they offered to print the fourth one for free, thanks to my relentless threats and complaints.

Martyrdom Street

There's a framed picture of Ali's ex-wife and son on the windowsill. In the photo they're sitting on a swing holding ice cream cones in their hands. "Why did you divorce?" I ask and feel him stiffen. "Not now," he answers. He continues rubbing my back in slow vertical movements, and I snuggle closer to him on the couch.

"When then?" I press.

"Soon," he promises.

Watering the flowers.

I can't decide whether my secrecy bothers him, even though he's used to hiding things about his life. For a time, he hid his profession from his parents. They considered his foreign wife a disgrace to the family. At the same time, they couldn't tolerate his profession. Fashion is acceptable for women, but men have to choose a respectable profession, not something frilly like fashion. Suddenly Ali laughs out loud. He delights at the thought of introducing me to people. "You're twenty-five, right?" he asks. I nod. Then he volunteers his age: "I'm forty-seven." He looks at me, waiting for a reaction, and I say what comes naturally to my mind: "You don't look that old." As I say it, I wonder whether I should have held back, but Ali doesn't seem offended by the candor. In fact, he looks slightly pleased. "My colleagues would be green with envy," he says with a thrill.

We kiss each other wildly on the couch. With Ali I can't stop myself the way I can with Fereydun. It gets harder every time. I like his touch on my flesh. His hands. The gray curls under his arms. His warmth next to my head. No. Stop. I leave the couch and begin to pack my bag. My clothes smell of hazelnut coffee beans, his favorite coffee flavor.

The flood is sinking the house.

"Don't run off," he says.

His hands outline my body, and I suck in my stomach.

"I have to," I say. "Tomorrow?"

"I can't. I'm meeting a student. I'll call you."

Ali zips the bag shut for me. I look into his deep brown eyes, the thin lines around them, and they remind me of something I've seen before somewhere in my life. Somewhere distant and bleak in the past. For the moment we are locked in time and space, but the future is just around the corner. Vague and anonymous. Like him. Like me. Like the woman pinned on his wall.

The Sand Castle

Fatemeh

A pigeon sits on an elm tree staring at me. I wonder what he sees. Maybe like everyone else the first thing he notices about me is my gnarled hand, is the way my fingers stretch out in a slow, contorted motion, struggling to straighten themselves out. But the more I stretch them, the more they curve inward toward my palm, and I stop struggling. My fingers fall to my side again, lifeless. As I put on my gloves to hail a cab, the pigeon shakes his head and looks away the way polite people do at parties after they acknowledge my hand.

If Muhsin had married his second wife after the accident, I could have blamed my marital problems on the injury and disfigurement. But failed marriages rarely have such simple explanations. Nasrin doesn't suspect a thing. Yesterday, in the kitchen, I wanted to tell her about Afsaneh, the opium, the prison days. But she seems so distant, preoccupied, so removed from the present.

Who is Afsaneh?

She was somebody I'd met time and again at parties, someone I'd run into at the department store or the deli. But I never noticed her until she became a part of my life. There was nothing particularly gripping about her. No stunning looks, no unrivaled intellect. In fact, she's ordinary, almost as ordinary as me. Only several years younger. One summer, as they were driving back from the shore, Afsaneh and her young husband got in a car accident. Afsaneh escaped with minor injuries, but her husband died instantly. Rumor has it that the collision occurred while the two were fighting over the custody of their son. Apparently, Afsaneh's husband had wanted a divorce.

Afsaneh started working at Muhsin's office just after her husband's death. She had a degree in the technical sciences and became the office manager. When

I look back, I hardly remember a time when he mentioned her. Usually, she came up only in passing: "Tomorrow, I'll ask Afsaneh to send a letter," or "I was talking on the phone and Afsaneh brought me some tea." Whenever we'd entertain Muhsin's colleagues at home, I'd insist that he invite Afsaneh, and she often appeared in simple but elegant European suits. At those dinners Afsaneh didn't talk much. She preferred leafing through magazines and sometimes helping out in the kitchen. Those gatherings, though at the time insignificant, have become engraved in my mind. They were the only times I interacted with Afsaneh. Were there obvious clues that I'd overlooked? Furtive glances between her and Muhsin? Brief moments alone in Nasrin's room?

I can't remember any. I'm not even sure if the passion between them had surfaced then. Maybe it was months later, in a solitary corner of the office, or at a mutual friend's house—a place from which I was intentionally absent. Their encounters, however frequent, must have been of short duration. At first, Muhsin always spent his evenings and weekends at home—if not with me, then at least beside me.

I never asked him about the affair or the marriage. After my accident, Muhsin broached the subject himself, although in my head I'd already pictured it all. I'd imagine him lying beside her, naked, gently caressing her back the way he did mine on our wedding night. I'd imagine her showing Muhsin pictures of her son. We never had a son. Again Muhsin disappointed me. Theirs was a hackneyed story. The tryst began a week or two after he'd been suspended from the university. I listened intently to his reminiscences, catching the occasional smiles that crept across his face when he'd mention her name. But why marriage, I asked. Wasn't an affair enough? That would have been so much more discreet, less serious. "She insisted," Muhsin justified. Then to absolve himself, he added, "Anyhow, it's sanctioned by your Islam." But this was an unbeliever's Islam. His affair hadn't begun because politics had intruded into our lives. We'd forced the barrier ourselves.

Nasrin

Waves wash away Hamid's footprints in the sand. He wanders toward the dregs of a wooden boat, and I follow him. It's early in the morning, and except for our presence, the beach is devoid of human life.

The Sand Castle

"How did you find this place?" I ask. He doesn't answer. I repeat the question, this time with an edge in my voice.

"My college roommate," he says. "He spent his summers here. Do you like it?"

"Yes," I lie.

"I'm glad," he continues, staring at the sky. "I thought you would."

I don't know what Hamid sees beyond the thick clouds. The sky makes me impatient. Its gray expanse confines the coast, closing off the ocean. I'd have preferred somewhere far south instead of this abandoned New Jersey resort. Most of the stores are out of business. Even the residential block contains more "For Sale" signs than it does inhabitants.

"Did your mother object to your coming?" he asks. He reaches for my arm as we walk along the beach.

"No," I say. "Why should she?"

He smiles and squeezes my hand.

A seagull's cries echo in the air as we reach the broken boat. Cycles of rain and wind have evened out the edges of its scattered boards. Though the enamel has been stripped off the exterior, three letters painted in red remain legible. H-R-M. I try to make out their meaning: Harmony. Heirloom. Harem. But I can't decide which sounds best to my ears. We climb into the boat's interior. A flattened life support jacket sags in a corner. Two yellow ropes dangle from the side of the boat, their braids damp and unraveled. Underneath the seat cushion there's a plastic bag, but when I look inside, I find nothing. "Disappointed?" Hamid asks. I nod. I'm disappointed that the bag contains no hints about the owners of the boat, that its past remains as mysterious to me as its present.

"I wonder why it's here," he comments.

"Who knows," I say.

"These beaches are usually free of debris."

"Maybe this is a private beach," I add.

"Maybe. But I didn't see any signs."

Hamid descends from the boat and chooses a suitable position for himself on the ground. He bends over slightly to begin digging, and the moistened sand quickly takes form in his hands. "Come here," he says, creating a small sandy hill near the boat. "In a minute," I answer, looking around. I try to imagine Hamid as a young boy, free of his guarded emotions and bureaucratic aphorisms, playing on the shores of the Caspian Sea. Instead, I see the placid waters of the sea repelling him away. I leave the boat to join Hamid. The earth cools my skin as I remove my leather gloves and start digging. My hands follow Hamid's and I let him direct our movements. This is the first time I've seen him in casual clothes, unshaven and soiled. His hair, though still moussed, has fallen out of place.

"What are we building?" I ask.

"Guess."

"I don't know. A tunnel."

"Wrong. Guess again."

"A dungeon."

"Close . . ."

"Oh, forget it," I say. "I'll just wait and see."

Driving up to the shore was Hamid's idea. I didn't know he'd be bringing me here, although I should've expected it. This was his way of making up for the Dallas. I can't say I was thrilled about coming, remembering the many lackluster dinners we'd already shared together. Dinners that showed we had nothing in common other than the same New Year. He likes pop music, I like jazz; he aims high, I underachieve; he reads the business section of the newspaper, I throw the business section away and save the rest. But here, away from the pressures of the city, it may still be possible to find something more.

"Remember?" I ask, taking a break from the digging.

"What?"

"That summer at the shore," I say, removing sand from his forehead.

"Uh huh," Hamid mumbles.

"We went to that old cottage."

I can tell that Hamid is neither listening nor remembering. He focuses solely on his digging, reaching deeper and deeper into the sand, as though convinced that his search will lead to some overwhelming discovery. But there is nothing hidden beneath the ground, not even a single seashell. For miles and miles, the oceanfront extends to the coast, barren, without a seashell in sight.

This isn't the way I remember the beaches in Iran. There, shells rose to the surface of the sea, leaving a busy trail along the shore. Most summers, tourists arrived to collect the rarest of seashells, except for one year when a drought kept the visitors away. That summer the sun raged overhead. There were no rains throughout the month of Mordad, just sparing drops of water then and again.

The Sand Castle

On the streets, girls complained about the blisters on their feet. "And the rice fields?" they grieved. "What will become of the harvest?"

That was the summer I met Hamid. At a luncheon he was introduced to me as a successful engineering student at Stanford, which at the time meant nothing to me. I was twelve. For the most part, the luncheon, like all the luncheons my mother dragged me to, was boring. To pass time, Yasaman and I decided to explore a secluded locale several homes away from my uncle's villa, and Hamid joined us. We meandered along a path strewn with thick weeds. The miasma of dying vegetation subdued the salty smell of the sea. Beyond this moribund terrain, we spotted a little cottage with broken windows. Hamid quietly opened the door, and we saw an old man draped in a navy robe, sitting cross-legged before a torn prayer rug. In slow motion he turned his head around in circles, speaking to himself.

"*La illaha illalla,*" he recited with each rotation of the head. As we listened to him, his iterations drew us into a trance. *La illaha illalla, la illaha illalla.* We linked hands and one by one repeated his phrase, "*La illaha illalla, la illaha illalla.*" When he noticed our voices outside the door, he stopped.

"Who is it?" he asked, rising from his seat.

"We didn't mean to disturb you," Hamid said, shutting the door behind us as we came in.

Scraps of a battered prayer book covered the wooden floor of the cottage. The dervish brushed aside fine specks of Caspian sand as he made room for us on his kelim, but the grains remained imprinted on the rug like nagging transgressions upon the mind.

"How did you find me?" the old man asked.

"By chance," Hamid answered.

"Have you ever heard her story?" the old man asked.

We shook our heads.

The old man then started to pray. His words rang familiar. They were prayers I'd heard before, but the dervish recited them to a different tune. He told us about a woman imprisoned at the bottom of the sea. As though awakened by the tale, the waters of the Caspian seemed to bubble for an instant. "She's listening," he said. "Can you hear?" We nodded and recited the *fatiha* after him. Then the dervish told us to leave. "Do not come back," he said. "You will not find me again." His words were prophetic, though we didn't realize it at the time. My uncle sold his villa that year and we never visited the Caspian shore again.

"I wonder what happened to that dervish," I say.

"Who?" Hamid asks.

"Never mind," I say. I knew he hadn't remembered.

Hamid sculpts the sand with moist fragments of wood, smoothing over bumps and carving angular indentations. The amorphous clod of earth in his hands has gained life. I recognize what he is building now. Something predictable but regal. The form expands, acquiring the rugged features of a stately edifice— majestic, ageless, and reaching splendidly toward the sky. He does not notice that I've moved out of his way until I begin etching stick figures with curled hair in poor imitation of the ruins of Parsa.

"It's finished," he announces. "What do you think?"

Hamid climbs inside the boat behind me to get a better view. I stand next to him, on top of the life jacket, watching him admire his artwork, and for a minute I ask myself whether life with him will be as horrendous as I've envisioned it. Maybe I haven't given him, or my fate, a chance. In that minute, Hamid kisses me. I close my eyes and for once try to welcome the intimacy. I imagine us sailing away upon this boat, somewhere distant and warm, but his touch constricts my breathing, and I feel faint. Before me I see the shadow of a woman. I can't tell who she is but she looks familiar. Gently, she runs her hands across my face until I can breathe again. When I open my eyes, I watch the waves crest onto the shore. Hamid stares at me unaware that a wave has flooded his sandcastle.

Yasaman

A lanky woman prances around half-naked backstage. Someone screams for coffee, while another complains about a zipper that refuses to shut. Finally, the event planner presses the "play" button on the stereo. Music fills the auditorium of the institute, and glamorous student models march on stage to begin the fashion show. My designs are next. The female judge in the third seat from the left fidgets in the green leather chair. She is vice president of Ramblers, the most popular teenage line of sportswear. I wonder if she'll like my collection even though my sportswear fashions are still kind of dressy—more for young business professionals than for teenagers at school. Still, Ali is convinced that my work will attract one of Fashion Avenue's executives, especially my "oriental" patterns, the long, dark taffeta skirts and tapestry-styled dresses. Fereydun probably doesn't even remember about my fashion show. I don't expect to find him here.

"How does this work?" a model asks, waving a red shawl.

I drape the shawl on her shoulders and tuck its edges under her black belt. My models, Anna and Claudia, spent the last two afternoons practicing a model's walk at the boutique. A week ago we met at Ali's apartment to watch a video of last year's student fashion show. Right now, Claudia claims a corner of the large mirror in the dressing room to inspect her braid. Without knowing how, I find myself putting makeup on a woman I've never met before. At the sound of Madonna's "Get into the Groove," Anna marches on stage, and I stand next to the curtain to watch. She walks cautiously in a two-buckled shoe and stares at the walls instead of the audience, but she doesn't trip. At the end of the walkway she places her hands on her hips and turns around twice, accentuating the tight leather miniskirt and silk sweater. As Anna exits, Claudia walks onto the runway. She holds her head high and flaunts one of my casual evening wear designs. This is a simple black dress with gold-rimmed, satin-coated buttons coming down the middle. She is holding a white rose in one hand. When she throws the rose to the crowd, the auditorium fills with applause and loud cheers. Claudia is a natural.

"It's a hit," Ali says, surprising me from behind.

I'm not sure, but I feel tender toward him. I want to thank him for telling me to participate. Instead, I ask him to meet me in the evening after the show. When no one is looking, he kisses me and walks away.

"How did we do?" Claudia asks, as she removes her high-heeled shoes and collapses on a chair to remove the thick stage makeup on her face.

"You were great," I say, although Claudia is preoccupied with the propositions being made to her by a well-known agent. Several minutes later, the judges make their decisions, and the prizes are distributed. The auditorium breaks into another round of applause. Claudia receives a first-place award as the outstanding student model of the fashion show. She approaches me with a hug and a token "I think you should have won." We mingle briefly among the agents and the audience, but mostly I want to find Ali. I see him walk toward me from the front of the room with a coffee in hand. "For you," he offers, giving me the drink. Then he introduces me to some coworkers. But the auditorium is getting crowded, and more than anything I want to leave.

"Are you all right?" he asks.

I nod and encourage him to socialize with his colleagues. When an agent seizes Ali by the sleeve to impart private information, I make a quick exit and try to stop the stinging in my stomach.

The man by the pretzel stand stares when he sees Ali and me walk hand in hand. Hoping to hide his curiosity, he pretends to look beyond us at the fluorescent bar lights that read "Open" and "Heineken." I ask Ali if he knows the man. Ali shakes his head. People often stare at us in public. To the outside world we must look strangely incongruous, he with his gray, thinning hair and me with my youthful complexion. They look once. Then they look again, just to be sure. There is no mistaking it. When they see our entwined hands, they know that we are not father and daughter. Their glances seem to ask, "What do you see in each other?" Or "Do you want to call my shrink?"

Ali and I don't do this often—walk in the streets of New York before 11 P.M. We are nearing pier 17 along the South Street Seaport. It has started to snow outside, and chances of running into Iranians we know here are slim. The judgment of strangers seems easier to endure than the censure of friends and family. We walk slowly on the sidewalk, avoiding thick patches of ice. On a summer afternoon, young business professionals and college interns people the restaurants and the stores. Tonight, the pier is mostly empty. A waiter stands outside of a cafe, drying his hands on a wait apron. As we walk by, he invites us in, but we move on.

We sit on the edge of the water catching snowflakes in our palms. The dark waves billow and crash against the sides of the wooden pier. We are not in the mood for a rowdy snowball fight—just a quiet moment alone in public. "I never appreciated snow until I moved to America," he says, burying his left hand in the right pocket of my coat. He relates short anecdotes about skiing trips with his son, who lives with his mother in France. "Last year, he broke his leg when I took him to Tahoe, and I never heard the end of it from Belle," he explains. Belle is short for Isabelle, Ali's ex-wife.

"What's wrong?" he asks when I don't respond.

"I didn't win," I say. "Are you disappointed?"

"Of course not. You did great."

"Was she a student of yours? The one who won?"

"Theresa?"

"Yeah. So what."

He takes me into his arms, and we embrace quietly. I slip my hand into his pocket to absorb his warmth. Though I've never felt such passion for a man before, the closeness unsettles. Then Ali says, "I don't always do this," he says. "Really." I wait for him to continue. "Go out with younger women, I mean."

The street lamps light up the surface of the water. For a moment I think I recognize a man's face. I search for him under the dark waters, but when I look again, the image is gone. Ripples cover the surface of the river, spreading out like a peacock opening its feathers. I listen to Ali, intoxicated by his words. His whispers. His promises. "Love? Yes, yes. I believe you," I say. We both sound desperate. Dependent, even. I let Ali pull me tightly toward him and kiss me more until the whistle of a nearby ship awakens the old man in my head.

Maybe Mendelssohn

Fatemeh

A man wearing a ski hat and thick gloves runs down a dirt trail. Toward the main yard, a group of schoolchildren awaits a tour of the surroundings. I enter the botanical garden from the left entrance. Next to me, a little girl looks at the tropical flowers at her side, but as she reaches for the petals, she's cautioned to stop. I try to appear inconspicuous, but I listen carefully to the guide, who labels the various species of flowers around us. "These are my . . . something, scor . . . something," he says, and the kids laugh when they hear the Latin name. "We call them forget-me-nots."

The schoolchildren gather outside a food stand to buy lunch. At the teacher's request they link arms, like a human locomotive, waiting for her orders. I find an empty bench nearby and sit down to read a book. From time to time, passersby drift into the botanical garden to eat lunch in the sun. I make room for a woman and her two boys on the bench.

A water fountain stands in the center of the yard where we are sitting. Though the fountain is dry, the children are attracted to it. They grab their sandwiches from the bench and run along its edges. "Be careful," their mother yells behind them. As they run around the fountain, their laughter grows animated, and I find myself drawn to their antics. One of them catches a baby frog and proudly presents the prize to his mother. "Let him go," she says sternly. Reluctantly, the boy lets the tiny frog leap out of his palm. Then the mother gathers their belongings and the trio marches out the gate. As they leave, I look around for the troupe of young students, but they too have gone. Like my garden, the courtyard longs for the company of laughing children. But I can sense that Nasrin has not embraced motherhood.

Maybe Mendelssohn

While the girls are at work, I prepare supper. Despite the amenities of my lifestyle here—no coupons, no long lines, no Komiteh—I don't belong. Even in the elevator, people's eyes seem to follow me. I see women with outfits worth more than my husband's biennial salary. They stare and take mental notes of my outdated skirts, and I return their gaze with calm. Women like that don't belong in Iran, women who have not known the dual responsibilities of family and war.

During wartime even something as basic showering is an extravagance. To conserve energy, the government obliges the country to endure daily power failures that last up to six hours. Warm water flows out of the faucet from dusk to dawn, when citizens least require it. Blackouts last longer than the night. Scant items of produce acquired after a day-long wait in the winding queues outside a grocery store wilt in the refrigerator. In shame, hands that discard the brown lettuce into the wastebasket stretch out for forgiveness. Without electricity or artificial light, home activities rapidly dwindle to none. Reading strains the eye. Vacuuming and laundry are relegated to nighttime chores. In the absence of bombing, only sleep sates any lingering passions.

Here, I can shower at any hour. I am enjoying the water, now, trickling down my back. Steam hugs my body the way clouds wrap around a plane. I massage my scalp slowly and scrub out the two-day-old grime. The citrus fragrance of the shampoo fills the tiny space between the shower curtain and the bathroom wall. Suds swirl down the drain, and I feel clean. I put on one of my progressive-looking suits. Muhsin would be pleased. When we'd attend receptions at the university, he liked choosing my outfits for me. He preferred me to wear Western clothes to impress the luminaries. Maybe he began noticing other women—the sort of women who flaunted their bodies and exceeded all bounds of propriety, wearing bikinis and drinking alcohol—when I insisted on wearing the veil during the revolution. These same women lived at the hairdresser's, molding an image invented by the Americans. In the sixties, they grew their hair long. In the seventies, they curled their hair. Although she never forgave me for telling her so, the Farrah Fawcett look didn't suit Zhaleh's mother, even after she dyed her hair blond. Such superficialities never belonged to *our* culture. They were imported values, sold to us at discounted rates in return for cheap oil.

Martyrdom Street

In protest, teenage boys learned to carry arms in the streets. Bazaar merchants raised their fists and closed shop, and bullets knocked down veiled women like sparrows out of trees. In downtown Tehran, the smell of rotting flesh became as commonplace as the scent of sour lemons. But we needed a revolution. We were becoming an immoral country. We were becoming little America.

Nasrin

The tempered melody of violins fills the café. Every few minutes a lonely customer next to my table gazes into the distance and listens. "More coffee?" the waiter asks. He anticipates my nod and aims for my cup. As I lean over to another table for sugar, the waiter approaches carrying a plastic tray with assortments of meat and potatoes. No drinks. Next to an order of steak fries, there are small bags of regular sugar and Sweet'N Low, which he drops on my table. I quickly open the bags of Sweet'N Low and pour them in my cup. I stir, unaware at first that I'm stirring to the rhythm of violins, and I smile in spite of myself as I recall a warm spring night in a dark forest.

Love didn't come to me in the typically fatalistic way I'd expected it. At first, it was random and repressed. Commonplace, even, like death. I recognized my deliberate attempts to run into Nicholas. The long hours in the library, the detours to the theater. It was all in me, the tumult and agitation of confused emotions. The feelings lingered like a childhood memory, becoming all-consuming and one-dimensional. I wanted him. I wanted to hold him, to touch him, to feel his body against mine. I felt dirty.

We met in a boring college history class on South Asia. Dr. Sanders, our professor, had spent years doing research there with his wife, a documentary filmmaker. He'd published two unremarked works while she'd completed a film on Afghan rebels during the Soviet occupation. One morning in class, Dr. Sanders showed excerpts of his wife's work, which focused less on the fighting and more on the way the villagers carried on with their daily tasks—fetching water and baking bread—while the war unfurled around them. Unfortunately, Dr. Sanders had to spoil the mood with his extraneous academic comments. As I counted the minutes until the end of his narrative, Nicholas stumbled into the classroom, thirty-five minutes late for lecture, and slipped into the seat closest to the door, the seat next to mine. We pretended not to notice each other.

Maybe Mendelssohn

Throughout the semester I saw Nicholas a few more times, usually outside Dr. Sanders's office, where we'd wait our turn to discuss paper topics with him. From those brief conversations, I learned that he was interested in architecture. But, more and more, he'd sit next to me during lectures. He'd borrow my pens. I'd glance at his notes. Before long, I was looking forward to meeting him every Tuesday and Thursday in class. At first, I ignored my feelings the way one overlooks a winter cold. In a week, I thought the physical manifestations—the fast heart beat, the sweaty palms, even the pain of not seeing him—would disappear. But the cold turned to pneumonia. The more I ignored it, the worse I felt.

Then one night Nicholas came searching for me in my dorm room. It was a weekend night, so I didn't feel bound by my books. Nicholas was wearing faded jeans and a tie-dyed T-shirt. When he knocked on my door, he became uncharacteristically shy and polite. "I didn't mean to bother you," he said. When he saw how eagerly I greeted him, he added, "I was just wondering if you wanted to go for a short walk."

We wandered toward the woods on the outskirts of the campus. An outdoor theater had been built there, just before the cross-country course began. Everything seemed a little cryptic. There was no moon. No street lamps, either. Other than headlights on stray cars, the theater creaked in darkness. I held Nicholas's hand, and we climbed down the steep stairs that led to the front of the stage. From his backpack he pulled out an empty champagne bottle with a candle in it. He lit the candle and placed the bottle on the gravel.

"This is where we rehearse," he explained. Nicholas was directing a one-act play about a father and son on the road to California. "Will you come to see it?" he asked. I nodded. In fact, I was dying to see it. We sat on the sandy ground with the champagne bottle between us, listening to the crickets fill our silence. Nicholas lit a cigarette and began to talk about himself. About how his parents divorced when he was nine, how his younger brother was expelled from prep school for smoking pot, and how he took a year off before college to go biking in Europe. Altogether, experiences unfamiliar to me. When he was done, he waited for me to continue, but instead our faces came close together and we kissed. It was a soft kiss, almost unexpected, that lasted for barely a minute. When it was over, we pretended it hadn't happened.

The next night Nicholas called and invited me to his room. As soon as I walked in, Nicholas rushed to conceal the clutter. "Sorry," he said, straightening out the hand-woven comforter on his bed and picking up books from the floor. "I'm genetically programmed to be messy." I laughed.

"I like it," I said.

"What? The comforter? It's Peruvian."

"No. The mess."

He stopped the rearranging and pulled a dossier off his shelf. It was a draft of his play. He gave to me and asked that I read it in my spare time. Then he pulled a CD off his shelf and dimmed the light before joining me on the couch. We listened quietly for awhile. Without realizing it, I fell asleep in his arms, lulled by the Mendelssohn.

A drop of sweat falls from the waiter's forehead onto the table and he quickly wipes it off with a napkin. "Ready to order now?" he asks. I remind him that I'm still waiting for someone, but he points to the line forming outside the door. "Lunch times are busy around here," he says, before grudgingly moving on to another customer.

"There you are," Nicholas says, as I order a Greek salad.

"You're late."

"I know. Sorry."

"I went ahead and ordered. Hope you don't mind."

Nicholas trips over his feet as he sits down. I can't stay angry with him for long. Nicholas is so disarmingly human. He stumbles, he eats with his hands, he wears tattered sweaters. When he's settled in his seat, Nicholas brandishes the menu until the waiter takes notice. "The soup and salad special, please," he orders.

"Is your coursework ending soon?" I ask.

He nods as he sips his water. "I can't wait, either."

We discuss Nicholas's schoolwork, his seminars, his professors' petty comments on his papers, his research trip to Italy. "It's a real honor," I say, "that they've asked you to go."

Nicholas lowers his head, reluctantly acknowledging the compliment. "Well, I wasn't really expecting it," he admits. As he unzips his navy blue backpack, I throw in a comment about my wedding plans. Though he's taken aback, Nicholas hides his surprise with a fake-sounding "That's great." I feign excitement about the wedding as well, and he adds, "Maybe your husband will let me visit sometime." We both laugh at his comment, knowing how Aesopian that request would be.

Maybe Mendelssohn

The waiter places the minestrone soup before Nicholas and brings my salad. As we eat, Nicholas's smile begins to fade, and I detect that something significant is about to happen. He brushes back his bangs and looks straight ahead, not exactly at me but through me, as though he were more interested in the coffee stains on the wall behind my head. "I have something for you," he declares, handing over a nicely wrapped package and card. "I know I've been a little moody, but, um, I just wanted to, um, I don't know . . . well, here, take this."

The package has the potpourri smell of a Hallmark store. When I rip the purple wrapping paper, I find a neatly bound manuscript. It's his one-act play, *California Caravan,* which he's dedicated to me. "I always wanted to do this," he explains, "especially when you came to see the play. But it just didn't seem right then." I nod. I want to respond, but I know my lips will quiver, and I don't want to cry.

"Don't worry," he continues, self-consciously, "it's not a way to win you over." He strokes my hand from across the table. He reaches over for a hug, and I rise up slightly to return his embrace. His arms linger around my neck, and I stay in my suspended position for a minute longer, holding on. Then Nicholas tears himself away.

"This means a lot to me," I finally manage when I sit back down on my seat. To diffuse the solemnity, Nicholas shifts the focus of our conversation, remarking on the "outrageous" bargain the travel agent offered him on his ticket to Italy.

"You all ready for your trip?" I ask, setting the manuscript on my lap.

"Yeah. In fact, I was wondering if you could stop by to take the things you'd left behind."

"I still have things at your place?" I ask.

"Yeah, you know, hair stuff, a Rolling Stones tape, some books."

"I don't know," I say.

Although Nicholas and I didn't date for long, I consider visiting his apartment an unwholesome move on my part, especially now that I'm engaged. "C'mon, Nasrin, it's no big deal," he insists. I feel slightly pressured, but maybe Nicholas is right. Visiting his apartment is no big deal, and after all, we've been friends for so long. "Okay, okay," I say, upon reconsideration. We split the bill, and Nicholas grabs his bag, following me out the door. His apartment is ten minutes away. When I walk in with him, his super recognizes me and offers a cordial hello.

Inside the apartment everything looks the same, except for the bags and suitcases on the floor. The black clock in the kitchen, still five minutes fast, hangs above the window. The ex-votos on the wall leading to his living room hang in their proper order: the wrinkled women at a bingo tournament followed by the children playing ball in an abandoned street corner. Even the handcrafted picture frame I gave Nicholas last Christmas sits on the speaker next to his bookcase. "Sorry about the mess," Nicholas says, bending down to fold old editions of the newspaper and carrying the pile into the kitchen.

"Here." He hands me a plastic bag filled with my belongings. "I think that's it."

"Thanks," I say.

"Want a beer?" he asks.

"Don't think so. I should be going."

But leaving is the last thought on my mind. I want to linger long enough to remember the familiarity of his couch, the titles on his bookshelf, and the symmetrical pattern of peacocks on his imitation Persian rug. "Whatever." He joins me in the living room, drinking his beer from the bottle. I'm not thirsty, but drinking will keep me from speaking.

"I'll have a Coke, though," I say.

Nicholas goes to the kitchen again to get the Coke.

"Here," he says, giving it to me.

The Coke bottle begins to thaw in my hands. I drink in quick small gulps. I feel restless. Even though I recognize the pastel pink walls, the red metallic cow that moos lamely, and the cadences of his rattling heaters, I somehow fail to fit into his decor.

"Want to listen to music?"

"Yeah, that would be nice."

Anything, I think, to enliven my reception in a room I once knew well. Nicholas walks to his cabinet to select a CD. Maybe Mendelssohn. He handles the disk gingerly, holding it by the edges in order not to place a fingerprint upon it. Then he asks about my mother and my wedding plans.

"Maman has been working overtime. She's amazing."

"I can imagine," he says. "Want anything else?"

"No, thanks," I say. "We just had lunch."

He rises to open a bag of nachos for himself.

"Is someone going to sublet your apartment?" I ask.

"Yeah."

"That must be a relief."

Maybe Mendelssohn

"It is, actually. I'd hate to waste money on it."

I shift in my seat and take another sip of Coke.

"You've hardly touched it," he comments.

"I'm a slow drinker, you know that."

"I know."

We both stop talking. I flip through the latest edition of his *Economist,* pretending to skim an article on Bosnia. Nicholas watches me, anticipating a comment. "This is weird," I finally blurt out, imagining myself a sixteen-year-old again.

"Why?"

"I don't know, it just is." I focus on the bronze paper wrapper that I've scratched off the beer bottle. Nicholas leans back on the couch, closing his eyes for a moment. "What am I doing here, Nicholas?" The question, I am sure, is also on his mind.

"I don't know," he says.

But we both know. He leans forward toward me, and we start to kiss. At first, we miss, but then, when everything begins to feel familiar, we kiss more. His hands grow warm and secure, and I let my fingers run through his hair. His blond head feels slippery and clean—all natural, with no mousse or gel gluing the strands together. "This isn't right," I say, but he quickly kisses my lips. We shift from the couch onto the carpeted floor. Nicholas's hands probe my body, he doesn't sense me stiffen and he continues.

The Mendelssohn has stopped playing. Some time ago we stopped taking notice of the music. Through the thin walls we listen to Nicholas's neighbors fighting over a late telephone bill. Nicholas and I remain intertwined on the floor without saying much. I hear him breathe on my neck, and he strokes my arms from time to time.

"Are you cold?" he asks.

"No. Are you?"

"No."

I lift my head from Nicholas's stomach and feel his sweat on my temple. He watches me walk into the kitchen. Nicholas's apartment seems more inviting now, and I pour myself a glass of orange juice. When I join him again, Nicholas is seated on the couch. The music starts again, and he pulls me gently toward him.

"Are you really getting married in two months?"

"I guess," I say.

I bend down to straighten my pleated black skirt.

"Are you going to hate me after this?" he asks.

"No," I say. "Are you?"

"No."

He hands me my sweater.

"What time is it?"

Nicholas reaches for his watch and answers, "Five after six." I'm late. I have to meet Hamid for dinner. I decide to take the stairs to the lobby. I walk fast, hoping to avoid the super. I'm sure he won't be able to tell, so I put my head down and walk out the door. A dim winter sunlight that threatens to fade behind afternoon clouds lingers outside. I don't look back. I walk through as many red lights as possible without killing myself. I don't feel sorry, but I can't stop thinking about Hamid. He'd never understand.

"What?"

"I said, do you want your package?" the doorman asks, when I'm in our building.

"Sure." He hands me a small box, and I step into the elevator. I stare at myself in the mirror. Loose strands of hair jut out in places, and I reconfigure my braid. My lips and cheeks aren't too red. My skirt hasn't acquired too many suspicious wrinkles. As I walk inside the apartment, Maman approaches to greet me. Do I smell like aftershave?

"How was lunch?" she asks.

"Fine."

Maman can't tell. I'm sure of it. She talks about Oprah Winfrey and youth violence in America. Then she asks me to move the furniture for the party in order to give the apartment a more spacious look. "Just a second," I say. I go into the bedroom and change. I hide the play Nicholas gave me under the bed and wear a new outfit. Pants instead of a skirt and a sweater instead of a cardigan. This way nobody will be able to tell.

Yasaman

Nobody remembers today. In the morning I woke up wondering whether some-one would mention it. Instead, I only heard Nasrin's alarm clock buzz for five minutes. Hers isn't one of those powerful alarms with a snooze button. It's a junk piece she winds up every night before going to sleep. Nasrin doesn't believe in keeping up with technology. Mrs. Gilani was already up and making breakfast. The television was on, too, and for a while I watched the news, which consisted of the usual list of violent crimes. A rape here, a murder there. A child pushed onto the subway tracks. Eventually, I switched the channel to *Good Morning America* to listen to an interview with Ivana Trump. "Who's that?" Mrs. Gilani asked, not recognizing the blond on the television set. Before I could respond, she quickly made the connection between Ivana and "that tall, gold building" that had the same name, the Trump Tower.

No. All in all, it's been a normal day. Nobody has mentioned a thing about it. Mrs. Gilani is cleaning, as usual. "I don't mind," she says with a smile when I ask her to stop. She continues rearranging the pots and pans: "Pyrex on top, brass on the bottom." But her movements have slowed down. It's the hand, the left hand she kept hidden the first night. The hand still works, but her fingers have an arthritic twist, refusing to straighten out, like a stubborn wrinkle on a linen skirt.

Outside, the weather is just cold and sunny enough for late February. I am in no mood to stay in the house. Mrs. Gilani will want to chat about the engagement party, and soon, the conversation will revert to when I will find myself a husband. This year I decide not to wear black. I put on a long, blue-green skirt that arrived in my boutique yesterday from Milan with a sweater the same shade of blue as the skirt. The skirt feels tight, and when I see myself in the mirror, I look heavy. Between my ribs, a small pocket of fat clings to my stomach, and I quickly run to the bathroom. I don't want Fereydun to feel the fat on me.

"Where are you off to?" Mrs. Gilani asks.

"To a fashion show," I lie.

I walk for thirty blocks until I reach an old church downtown that Fereydun and I like to visit. There are no mosques near us, so I make do with what is available. I pretend to be Christian. Well, not exactly. I just borrow the Christian house of worship, but everything I do inside a church is downright Muslim. I recite the prayers my grandmother taught me in Arabic, although I don't understand what I'm saying.

Migrating clouds shelter the sun, and for an instant the church loses its luster. A black clock attached to the spire is no longer capable of telling time. Its rusty hands have frozen on the roman numerals two and seven. This church is less of a tourist attraction than St. Patrick's Cathedral. Here, people don't snap pictures or giddily march up and down the aisles to peer at the artwork.

A man in the front row gazes at the ceiling. Somewhere in the middle, two old women kneel before Christ. Toward the back a girl just sobs, staring straight ahead. I decide to sit on the other side of the aisle from the young woman. I open one of the psalm books even though I can't read music but I quickly feel sacrilegious and shut the book. A breeze sails through the open door of the church entrance. In unison, the flames lean to the right and left like a troupe of ballerinas. The stained-glass windows absorb their shimmer, and Mary's tunic reflects their crimson tones. Church colors are dark and earthy, unlike the colors of a mosque. The deep green tunics and the russet robes of the saints render Christ's suffering palpable even for a Muslim.

I light another candle and repeat a prayer. Then I slip a fifty-dollar bill in the donation slot before walking outside. The brightness hurts my eyes, and I put on my sunglasses. Though the streets around the church are busy, the air is quiet in the graveyard. Of all the graveyards I have surveyed in New York, this one is my favorite because it contains a small rose garden. Sometimes when I need ideas for fabrics or designs, I come here with a large notebook and color pencils to sketch the kind of spring this year's line might bring. For a boisterous spring, I draw a baby-doll dress that falls just above the knees with small flowers of mustard yellow or turquoise blue. For a more subdued look, I pencil in a navy cotton skirt sprinkled with lilacs and orange petals.

Today, I draw random objects. A waterhose. Ants. A man's long-sleeved shirt. Together, the figures don't amount to much. I rip the drawings from my notebook and throw them in the garbage bin. After smoking my third cigarette, I decide to walk around the graveyard. I take an inventory of all the tombstones, and next to the side entrance to the cemetery I choose my favorite. Small arcs are carved around the top of the concrete gravestone. I run my hands against the smooth surface of the rock. The soft sensation roughens only when my fingers graze the perfectly chiseled inscription in the center of the stone. February 20—the twelfth anniversary of my father's death. He died on a sunny afternoon with a crooked smile on his face, lying next to a pot of hyacinths with two streaks of blood rolling down the sides of his mouth.

I have never seen his real grave. We had his body interred in a small village cemetery near Tehran a day before leaving the country. A local mullah, whom we obtained on short notice, came and mumbled a few prayers, while a carpenter chopped a piece of wood and painted my father's name as well as some Qur'anic verses on it. The whole affair lasted about ten minutes. No one knew to attend the ceremony, since it was held in secret. After that speedy service, we never found the time to mourn my father's death, although my grandmother did offer to buy his real tombstone and insure its proper installation. We fled, fearing the killings after the revolution. The Tehran daily newspaper featured celebratory articles about the people executed by the government each morning. A gory photograph and a distorted biographical caption usually accompanied the news columns. For variety's sake, the newspapers would even display before-and-after portraits: Mr. So-and-so as minister in 1977 regaling Jimmy Carter at an official dinner party followed by a repentant picture of Mr. So-and-so in 1979 lying in the sea of his own infidel blood.

The radio stations were hardly a diversion. I stopped listening when the government prefaced the world news hour with an enumeration of the executions taken place earlier that morning. The announcer would begin with his customary *"Bismillah al-rahman al-rahim"* and then he'd read off the names of the executed. His recitation reminded me of roll call. Only nobody was alive to yell "present."

We packed a lifetime's worth of belongings into two suitcases and handbags and left without saying good-bye to anybody—not even our uncles, aunts, or cousins. There was our house, which my grandmother decided to live in, and a summer villa, which was rented out to a friend. Everything else we owned was located outside the country. My mother hired two chauffeurs who'd previously been employed by our family to drive us to the border of Iran and Turkey. Apparently, they'd already successfully smuggled out a number of political fugitives, and they owed us a favor. Years ago, these men had been arrested for dealing drugs and my father had bailed them out. We traveled at night to be inconspicuous and hid the car during the daytime in remote homes along the way where our drivers had acquaintances. At every stop, my mother doled out hefty sums of cash to keep our hosts happy, knowing all along that there were no guarantees. Anyone at any time could turn against us, especially at the border, but nobody even bothered to search our luggage, passports, or plane tickets. Nothing. When we crossed the line into freedom, it was three o'clock in the morning Turkish time.

Outside the customs building, the guards handed us a schedule. The earliest bus would not arrive until the morning. There were no hotels nearby, just a bar on the other side of the street. The smoke of cheap cigarettes clouded the barroom, but we entered anyhow to buy cold sodas. As my mother stood at the counter, a soldier approached her and offered to buy our drinks. The soldier would not go away even after my mother bought the sodas herself. He rubbed his body against hers, and his hands wandered all over her skirt. My mother pushed him back and walked quickly toward our booth. But he followed her there, and in front of me he started to fondle her breasts. I screamed, the only thing I knew to do, but that didn't deter him, either. I couldn't believe it. I screamed again, this time an octave louder, and three men came to the table. They muttered something to the soldier and he eventually walked away. We spent the night wide awake at the bar until the buses arrived.

My mother has never acknowledged my father's death. Maybe she blames him for what happened to her in that bar. Maybe it's just easier to forget. But I can't. That's the difference between a spouse and a child. A wife or husband can always remarry, but you can never find another parent. I decided not to wear black this year because black has lost all meaning. Black is just another color and the anniversary of his death is just another day. The past does not disappear after I take off my black clothes or after the day ends. Sadness like this occurs in cycles, in short seasonal cycles, never in leap years. Seasonal sadness is hard to evade. It creeps in everywhere like summer heat in an un-air-conditioned home. No matter what you wear, or where you sleep, it lingers. A hole digs into my stomach and I wait until the next cycle begins.

People arrive for the free noontime concert at the church. I take one last glance at that tombstone. If given the choice, the gravestone I'd have ordered for my father would have resembled this, except instead of the concrete, I would have chosen marble, although marble isn't customary. I asked my grandmother to take a photo of my father's actual grave, but she refused, considering my request too morbid. Another time, I suggested transferring his remains to America, but again she refused, claiming his heart lived in Iran. Funny, I thought. His flesh and blood are in America, but his heart lives in Iran. We let him stay.

Maybe Mendelssohn

A homeless man looks on as I zip up my purse. "Some change, miss?" he asks. I dig inside my coat pocket and drop three quarters, two pennies, and a dime in his hands. I make sure not to touch him because of AIDS. You never know who might be infected. An Asian girl sits next to a bucket of flowers outside the deli across from the church. She sips coffee while reading a newspaper. Though the flowers have shriveled petals and curled leaves, I buy a dozen wilted roses. There are no other florists in the neighborhood. As I place the flowers on the tombstone, I wonder what that boy is doing today—he's probably a grown man by now. I imagine short encounters with him. On the street. Inside a factory. Outside our home. Just to ask why.

Stolen Jewels

Fatemeh

At my parents' annual *rowzeh khani* during the holy month of Safar, a sage clergyman stopped me by the door to say, "No matter what happens, always follow the path of God." He wasn't the regular preacher who presided over our yearly religious congregation. Without an explanation, Hajj Agha lifted his hand, placed it on my forehead, and began to mutter long-winded verses. At first he made me feel guilty. I'd skipped my early afternoon prayer that day for a petty reason: to go to the public bath and wash up, not in order to attain divine cleanliness but to look good in front of my future mother-in-law, Fakhri Khanum. I was sure God had sent Hajj Agha as a warning and reminder that hell could greet me in this world as well as the next if I ignored my religious duties.

As he prepared to deliver his sermon, I assured Hajj Agha that I was a good Muslim, that I'd never missed a fast during Ramazan, and that I had every intention of going on the pilgrimage to Mecca once I got married. He smiled and said, "I know," which appeased my anxiety. Before entering the men's quarters, he added, "We're not meant to understand everything."

As tradition dictated, Hajj Agha recounted the heroic feats of the prophet's family during the sermon. He described Hazrat Ali's bravery—may he rest in peace—before the kafirs at the Battle of Uhud: "And the innocent Fatima, when she saw her great father, Hazrat Muhammad in pain, she nursed him throughout the night." He paused. "But it was God's will. Doom fell upon Mecca and Medina after the prophet's death . . ." At the sound of his sinister re-creation of this tragedy, Fakhri Khanum let out a loud snort and began to wail. *"Allahu Akbar,"* she said, counting her worry beads. My mother, who was sitting near by, jumped to her feet.

Stolen Jewels

"Here, have a cracker, have some sweets," she offered, hoping to muffle Fakhri Khanum's snorts. But nothing worked. Fakhri Khanum was in need of a good cry. She'd lost money on a piece of property somewhere on the outskirts of town.

Madar Joon told me to go outside and bring back two large bottles of rosewater. The door to our yard was open. On the street, people who'd been listening to the sermon from the loudspeakers came strolling into the yard to ask Hajj Agha for special prayers. An old woman with wrinkled cheeks held out her hands so I could sprinkle them with the blessed rosewater.

"Thank you," she said, rubbing the rosewater on her face. "May you get married soon."

A month later, I was engaged to Muhsin. I had known him for most of my life—we lived on the same street a few doors away—but we noticed each other for the first time at the library of the local university. I was checking out a history book, and he was returning a journal on politics. One day he put a note in my textbook and followed me home. It was impossible to have a courtship without involving the entire neighborhood. So Muhsin did everything the right way. He approached my parents and asked for my hand in marriage. We decided early on that we were in love, that our encounter was destiny, and that we were meant to spend the rest of our lives together. Things happened quickly between us. In the ensuing weeks, we had to readjust our lives to account for the changes.

Madar Joon invited Hajj Agha to preside at our wedding ceremony. After performing the rites of passage, he repeated his cryptic warnings. "Don't fight fate," he warned. What did he mean? Did he think my marriage was a mistake? Or was he alluding to some large philosophical truth that had eluded me? As my mother-in-law rubbed the henna in my hands on my wedding day, she whispered, "Be an obedient wife and bring us a son."

Everything seemed so simple. He liked the right side of the bed, while I preferred the left, and it turned out that we were both morning people. There was so much we wanted to learn about each other, we hardly had any time left for others. For the first few weeks, Muhsin seemed happy. Actually, now that I look back, he never mentioned anything other than how much he wanted to have a child with me. I became pregnant exactly a month after my wedding. My mother-in-law, overjoyed with the news, fell into a heavy stupor—later we discovered that she was suffering from a brain tumor—and about two weeks after our announcement she died in her sleep. Probably it worked out for the best, since my mother-in-law likely would have blamed the miscarriage on me. We lost the baby about as quickly as we had conceived it. Muhsin and I never dwelled on the loss of our first child. We accepted it as an event we were not meant to understand, just as Hajj Agha had warned.

Yasaman

An air of anticipation fills the apartment today. This is a mood that accompanies the execution of serious endeavors: projects on which one has toiled for months, in which one has invested time and ego, and which in the end demand independent life, like a fetus. Nasrin enters the room with a bouquet of tulips. She takes the flowers into the kitchen and trims each stem one by one like a seasoned gardener.

The living room is adorned with simple relics: an old tapestry, a bottle of rosewater, a crystal vase. But the chipped edges and faded inscriptions on these mementoes don't betray their histories. The crystal vase shimmers under the artificial light. I shine it gingerly, knowing it has not yet attained its full grandeur. For a second, I place its opening next to my ear as if it were a giant seashell, expecting to hear the calls of village gypsies. But I only hear an empty silence. Was this Ali's experience on his wedding day?

I hand the vase to Nasrin. She slowly approaches the table but doesn't notice the grocery bags in her path. Her mother pulls gently on the edges of the tablecloth to smooth away the creases before making a spot for the flowers on the table. As Nasrin loses her balance, the vase collides with the wooden table and disintegrates into a million different sparkling pieces. The shards sparkle under the light like the stolen jewels on a monarch's crown. We rush to Nasrin's side.

"No!" Mrs. Gilani exclaims.

"I'm sorry," Nasrin says.

We bend down to gather the angular pieces, but Mrs. Gilani pushes us away. She sits on the floor and stares at the remnants of the vase like a forlorn child whose toys have ceased to function. One by one she collects the shards, matching the figures and shapes, convinced that the future somehow depends upon it.

Nasrin

"I burned it! I burned it!" Yasaman yells.

Stolen Jewels

"What? Who's hurt?" Maman asks as she jerks her head up from the prayer rug.

"My outfit," Yasaman whines. She buries her head in the antique lace shirt she has burned while ironing. Maman takes the shirt from Yasaman to see if she can somehow salvage it. She turns the fabric from side to side, carefully examining the pattern under the light. The iron has left a rusty streak along the neckline, and the scorched lace threatens to fall apart in Maman's hands. The shirt is beyond repair.

"Come on," I say. "Let's find you something else."

We search through Yasaman's closet and find at least a dozen other suitable substitutes. I choose a silk dress. "How about this?" I propose, holding up the dress for Yasaman's inspection. She sulks. The silk just isn't the same as the antique lace. It makes her look fat. "Okay, what about this one?" I suggest, pointing to a simple skirt and shirt in an elegant red-and-black motif.

While Yasaman considers my second option, I put on my dress and fix my hair. Yasaman decides against the red-and-black outfit, opting instead for a low-cut purple shirt and tight black miniskirt, which exposes her long legs as well as the curves of her body. Maman stares at Yasaman as she zips up her skirt. When Yasaman enters the bathroom to apply her makeup, Maman whispers to me, "Do you think I should tell her to change?" I shake my head and remind my mother that miniskirts are legal here.

The doorman buzzes us from downstairs as I enter the living room. Within minutes, Hamid and his mother enter with a dozen red roses. Mrs. Goshayesh surveys the apartment from the corner of her eye and smiles, no doubt pleased by the number of expensive objects on display. "My sweet daughter," Mrs. Goshayesh exclaims, grabbing me and depositing two wet kisses on my cheeks. "Don't you look soooo pretty. I told everyone in Tehran I was adopting the most beautiful daughter-in-law around." I smile coyly, as I am supposed to do, and then go into the kitchen. Hamid follows there. As I reach for the jar of tea leaves, he removes a box from his left coat pocket.

"I have something for you," he declares. "My mother wants you to wear this tonight." It's a gold necklace. "It's gorgeous," I lie. Hamid offers to fasten the necklace for me, but I attach the clasp from behind myself. Then Hamid leads me to his mother to allow Mrs. Goshayesh to admire her gift. I lean over and thank my future mother-in-law with a kiss. "You shouldn't have," Maman remarks in a classic example of *ta'rof*. Maman actually expected such a gesture from Mrs. Goshayesh, but she *ta'rof*ed out of politeness and to evade the obvious. Satisfied by our reaction to the necklace, Mrs. Goshayesh takes a hearty sip of her tea and inquires about our preparations for the wedding. As Maman answers, I go to meet the other guests outside the apartment.

My elderly aunt and uncle from Brooklyn are the first ones to arrive, followed by Valerie, Yasaman's best friend. "We're very proud," my uncle offers, extending his hand for Maman to grasp. He is going blind. They have no children of their own, so they see me as one of their own.

"Hi, Uncle Abbas," I say. He gropes in midair for my face. When he finally grabs hold of it, he slobbers me with kisses. He asks to meet Hamid. "He's right here. Hamid, this is the uncle who raised me." I know how much Uncle Abbas appreciates this acknowledgment. Hamid shakes his hand, and I detect that my uncle has approved of Hamid, since he's still holding onto his hand. Uncle Abbas can tell a lot by a handshake. Clusters of people form in the living room, and I begin my rounds, dropping in from one conversation to the next. Valerie has struck up a dialogue with Fereydun and Parviz. With a vodka tonic in hand, Valerie waves to me. She stares at Parviz while he regales her with stories about his latest encounters with the former royal family.

"Congratulations," Fereydun offers when I approach them. He's recovered from the bullet wound and nearly suffocates me with the smell of his cologne as we exchange greetings. As usual, he's dressed impeccably, with his black hair greased back along his high forehead and a monarchist button pinned to his lapel. He talks about his success in raising money for the upcoming PERSIA art exhibition, and his friend Parviz joins in the conversation.

"How's school?" I ask Parviz.

Parviz studies law at Columbia. I understand his family facilitated his acceptance with connections or money or both. When he's not squandering his life in nightclubs, Parviz occupies himself with the loss of his family's illegitimate power and wealth. His political aspirations include attaining the post of prime minister in Iran. In fact, he belongs to an underground group of Iranian monarchists who remain loyal to the Pahlavi clan in exile. They orchestrate demonstrations in Washington and California, distribute leaflets among Iranians, and order monarchist pins, like the one Fereydun wears on his lapel, with the prerevolutionary Iranian flag as its emblem and an engraving that reads, "Iran shall never die."

"Inspiring," he replies in his usual pompous voice and inhales a large drag of his cigarette. "I tell you, I met His Imperial Majesty the Shah last week. He is going to return to Iran in six months," he confides. Parviz always claims to have "just met" with His Imperial Majesty about an impending coup. By now, his acquaintances know better than to take his political prognostications seriously. As I leave them for another crowd, guests continue to arrive. I stop in the kitchen momentarily and find my mother holding a large wooden ladle and looking more and more concerned about her meatballs and tomato sauce.

"Amir is looking for you," she comments. Amir, a second cousin on my mother's side, is the relative with whom I have the best rapport. His antics have made him either the subject of family canards or the envy of his cousins. After college, Amir insisted on pursuing avant-garde activities like traveling to the Third World to work for Mother Theresa. "I mean," my aunt used to say, "doesn't he realize that we're trying to get out of the Third World?" Amir's decision to grow a ponytail and pierce his left ear did not endear him to the family, either.

"Where is he?" I ask.

"I don't know. Probably near the bar," Maman jokes. The family also accuses Amir of being an alcoholic.

Mrs. Goshayesh enters the kitchen as I leave to find Amir. She inquires about the dinner menu and insists that my mother add more parsley to her Persian hamburgers. Maman calmly accepts her suggestion. I make sure to leave before she has an opportunity to talk to me and mingle with a covey of people near the bar. "Hope you don't mind," I hear Amir say, "I decided to bring one of my classmates along. This is Melissa." As Melissa greets us, she enunciates every word in a crisp academic voice. "Which one is the groom-to-be?" she asks. Her eyes search the room for the person she thinks is Hamid. "Over there." Amir points to the kitchen. Hamid notices Amir gesturing and walks toward us. *Che tori,* Agha," Amir offers, patting Hamid on the back.

"Did you find Amir?" Maman asks when I step into the kitchen.

"I found him," I say.

"Who's the American?" she asks.

"His girlfriend," I answer and Maman shakes her head.

The boisterous voice of a woman overpowers our conversation as I place a tray of rice with herbs on the dining room table. Mrs. Arezou has finally arrived. "Fatemeh joon," she exclaims in the same shrill, high-pitched voice that Mrs.

Goyashesh used upon arrival. "Where's the happy couple?" she asks, her eyes quickly sizing up my mother and the apartment. She removes her heavy mink coat and hands it to Hamid without even acknowledging him.

Mrs. Arezou is a family friend of my mother's from the prerevolutionary days. She and her sister grew up in a small city to the north of Tehran called Rasht, but they did not belong to the aristocratic land-owning families that controlled northern Iran. One generation back, they came from modest yet comfortable backgrounds, owning small pieces of land in local villages. After high school, they were married to eligible young men from the neighborhood. They produced kids while their husbands took advantage of the modernizing plutocracy that the shah had created. They became businessmen, forming monopolies in various markets. In the meantime, their wives became consumers of Western goods and values, looking down upon anything that was not "Made in USA." I never notice how beautiful my mother looks until I see her standing next to Mrs. Arezou, who after three facelifts and a nose job still is less attractive than Maman. Right then, I feel very glad that she is my mother and not Mrs. Arezou.

"I'm delighted you could make it," I ta'rof. "It's always such a pleasure to see you." These rehearsed responses flow out of my mouth tonight. I've heard so many, it doesn't take much effort to fabricate my own. Mrs. Arezou grins at my well-executed ta'rofs. Hers is one of those half smiles that famous people flash in front of television cameras to give lowly masses the impression that famous people truly can be warm and considerate on top of being famous.

A crowd of guests has already gathered around the table when Maman brings out the crispy portion of the rice. As Amir picks at the fresh tah diegh, Hamid and I invite the guests to serve themselves. "What have you done?" Mrs. Arezou exclaims when she observes the array of homemade dishes Maman has prepared. The table resembles an edible kaleidoscope, with colorful delectables piled from one end to the next. I start passing around the dishes while Hamid serves the drinks. This is solidarity, I think. We want to convince everyone, including our-selves, that we make a caring and affectionate couple.

Civilized people turn barbaric around food. My aunt forms two large heaps of rice and meat sauce, topped with chicken kebab and salad. Then she reaches across the table to claim her rightful share of pita bread and Bulgarian cheese. Since she cannot find any room on her plate for the bread, my aunt crumples the napkin in her one hand and uses the other to hang on tightly to the bread. As she walks across the room, a piece of saffroned chicken drops from her plate. She does not notice the missing chicken leg, but Amir reaches down to clean up the mess. Others join in once my aunt and uncle are seated in the living room.

When everyone is served, Hamid and I fill our plates. I sit next to my uncle from Brooklyn, who is straining his ears to listen to a political debate that has erupted between Parviz and Amir. They are known to get on each other's nerves.

"Quite frankly," Amir retorts, "I don't see what you're complaining about. It was your family's corruption that sent the rest of us here." Amir lacks the refined manners that Parviz's comfortable upbringing has bred. He does not believe in *ta'rof*ing. Once a phrase is transcribed in his head, Amir utters the thought without any editing.

"Well, if you're so unhappy here, why don't you go back?" Parviz responds. Parviz can't tolerate self-righteous liberal intellectuals, like Amir, who complain about everything, anything, and all governments. If the socialists are in power, they remonstrate against wasteful, inefficient bureaucracies. If the monarchists dominate, they protest against the arbitrary nature of justice and government. If the religious fundamentalists seize control, they condemn the intolerance toward secular value systems. Liberals, Parviz once told me, are nothing but a bunch of whiners. They criticize everything but offer nothing. Parviz votes Republican.

"Allah akbar," my uncle grumbles to himself, spitting out a chicken bone and pushing its remnants to the side of his plate. Hamid interjects, hoping to tone down the debate, but Parviz and Amir talk over him. In between spoonfuls of rice, he mutters underneath his breath, "Only an idiot would want the monarchy back."

"Allah akbar," my uncle repeats, his voice a pitch louder.

"Nothing is perfect," Parviz prefaces diplomatically, hoping to manipulate the conversation in another direction. It's obvious that he's preparing to deliver a long, boring speech. "At least under the shah there was economic development, more freedom for women, educational opportunities . . ."

"Corruption, repression, Western usurpation," Amir completes the sentence for him.

When Parviz looks away, Amir wiggles his tongue to shift a piece of rice stuck to his teeth. No one knows what political party Amir belongs to. He's too rational to be a religious fundamentalist, too egalitarian to be a monarchist, and too self-hating to be a nationalist. There's a brief lull in the conversation, and for a moment the only noise in the room comes from the clanking of forks and knives against the porcelain dinner plates. Then Amir says, "If it weren't for the CIA, we wouldn't be in this mess in the first place."

"*Allah akbar,*" my uncle explodes, his voice nearing a scream. "Why don't you young people talk about something else? We don't want indigestion tonight." My young cousins attempt to stifle their laughter. Uncle Abbas moves to the other side of the room to finish his meal in isolation. "They don't even let you eat in peace anymore," he mumbles to me.

Maman hovers around the room, filling our plates anew with rice and sauce. "Here, Amir, can I pour you some?" She dishes out the rice before Amir has a chance to respond. Melissa looks amused by the debate. This discussion, I'm sure, stimulated more thought than her graduate school seminars. At least for us the issues are real, not mere research topics. We've lived through the events she's read about. I wonder if Melissa, the only Westerner in the room and our token imperialist, feels hesitant about contributing to the discussion. When I ask about her views on Middle Eastern politics, she skillfully evades the subject.

As the debate subsides, I excuse myself to find a moment alone. The bedroom is disorderly and silent. No people, no *ta'rofs,* no debates. Just a heap of clothing and the smell of cigarettes. I open the window and sit on the edge of the sill. A cool breeze rolls in, slowly clearing my head. I tune in and out of the noise on the streets, brushing back strands of hair that have fallen across my cheek. Except for the patches of light from outside, the room is cloaked in darkness. Iran and its politics seem distant at the moment, as if they were never a part of my life.

When I return to the living room, Maman gathers everyone around. Mrs. Goshayesh makes a short speech to unify the guests and families, and then Hamid slips the engagement ring on my finger. Mrs. Arezou cranes her neck to see what Hamid has purchased. "Well, dear," Hamid says, emphasizing the *dear* now that he can legitimately express some affection, "may I take your other hand?" He reaches forward and gently kisses it. In Iran, we would still be flouting traditional Iranian engagement norms. But tonight no one lets on that we have transgressed the boundaries of wedding decorum, so eager are we to appear acclimated to the rules of exile dating. There is a brief round of applause and pot banging. Yasaman blares earsplitting Iranian wedding music from her stereo, while Fereydun, and now Amir, begin tapping the pots to the song's drumbeat.

Stolen Jewels

One by one, the guests come forward to congratulate us. They offer their best wishes for our happy life together. Someone has pulled out a camera, intent on using up a 36-exposure roll of film on us. I force myself to smile widely and to exchange looks of embarrassed affection with Hamid, although I don't want to commemorate this night forever.

Shooting Stars

Yasaman

"Do you want anything?" my store manager, Claudia, asks on her way out. Valerie calls out for a hot chocolate and I ask for an espresso. A small bell goes off when Claudia opens the door. Cold air creeps into the store, and Valerie and I huddle near a space heater. Wild winds holler outside the window. A woman wraps her coat tightly around her body, swaying from side to side. Across the street, a man chases his felt hat, and by the newsstand, another sips his warm cup of coffee. Today, passersby enter the store more for warmth than for shopping. This is a slow morning at the boutique.

"Will it snow tonight?" Valerie asks.

"I think so," I say.

"Why don't you close early then," she suggests, and I agree.

I open a small notebook to draw but fail to perceive the dimensions of the light. Instead, I watch as Valerie opens a box that has arrived from Milan. She rummages through the order until she finds a dress that she'd seen in the last issue of Italian *Vogue*. But she seems disappointed that the actual dress isn't as impressive as the advertisement. "I hope you don't lose money on it," she says. I assure her I won't. The dress is appropriate for any nightclub around here. I had even worn it at the fashion show.

"That was fun," Valerie says, referring to the fashion show as she carries a nude mannequin to an uncluttered corner of the store. "Everyone looked so glamorous."

I nod.

"How's Ali?" she asks, putting the dress on the mannequin.

I answer in a general way about his work.

"No, I mean you two," she probes.

"Fine," I say.

Valerie tries hard not to seem disappointed at my reticence. When she accepts that I don't want to pursue the subject, she starts talking about herself. I soon learn that she has planned a bicycle trip to Europe for the summer. France, Italy, and maybe Spain. We go through some invoices, and eventually Claudia returns with our drinks.

"It's freezing," she says.

Valerie takes her cappuccino and returns to the cashier's counter. I rush to answer the phone. It's my mother, calling from England. This is unlike her to phone in the early morning, London time. Usually, Maman prefers to call me in the midday, at home. "What's wrong?" I ask, anticipating the worst. There is nothing wrong. She just wants to speak to me, which is equally unusual. I ask when she will come to visit. She avoids the question and instead chats about my brother's current girlfriend. When she notices that I've lost interest, she admits that she will not be coming to New York this spring, as promised, and I recognize this as the real reason for her call.

"I'm going to Argentina," she reveals.

"What's there?" I ask, although I know.

She will visit Cesar but we don't discuss him, either. Cesar is a divorced heart surgeon with five children. During the year, he lives with my mother in London, even though she denies it. I don't know when or how they met. Maybe at a party. Or on an airplane. Or in a bar. He answered the phone once when I called. I pretended to be someone else.

"When will you be stopping here?"

"In the summer. July, I think."

Then she asks about the boutique and sounds surprised when I tell her that the store has made a profit. As I start to discuss our new line of sportswear, she cuts me off abruptly to attend to her cat. She sends me two kisses before getting off the line.

I decide to go for a short walk. The store is not busy, and two people can easily tend to the customers. From the windowsill, I take the pot of white hyacinths with me. I don't have a destination in mind. Before long, I find myself near the East River, walking into a stiff wind from the water. A gale knocks over a garbage bin, and two cans of Diet Coke roll down a narrow alley. The neighborhood seems grayer than I remember.

I call Ali on my cell phone. He's usually home at this hour.

No one answers, so I dial his office. There are voices in the background.

"I'm busy," he says. "I'll call you."

I walk to the edge of the river. The cold numbs my body and I stiffen like a child in deep shock. There's nobody here. I put the pot of hyacinths on the boardwalk. My stomach dilates as two fingers slip down my throat. I lean over the railing to watch the current and then empty my stomach. Sweat clings to my hair, and my face feels red. The smell of burnt leaves drifts overhead. A thin layer of ice cracks beneath my feet as I throw the pot of hyacinths in the water. Where will it end up? In innocent hands, along a country road, or at Ali's doorsteps?

Nasrin

The waste-infested lake looks as black as the petrol seeping out of Iran's oil wells. A blond-haired woman about my age lies prostrate on a bench writing in her dairy. Every few paragraphs, she lifts her head up to take a moment and breathe the air, overhear a private conversation, or record an impression. She notices me and smiles. I acknowledge her, too, before staring into the toxic lake again. Would Narcissus have loved this polluted vision of himself? Would he have jumped in or thought better of it?

An old violinist holds court and entertains the bystanders near the lake. He plays nostalgic Paganini for his fans who throw coins and dollar bills in his violin case in gratitude for the free performance. As I clap for him, I turn my head, half-expecting to find Nicholas. Instead, I see the blond taking notes in her diary.

Two preschool kids huddle closely on the steps where I am sitting. Their sentences are pieced together with long pauses and giggles. They point to a canoe carrying an elderly man and woman. When one of them begins to cry over a toy, I move away. I hope Hamid won't insist on starting a family soon. Fifth Avenue hums with enchanted tourists and creaky baby carriages. A well-dressed woman walks down the block at my speed. She picks up the pace to catch the green light but the woman does not hazard running in her high-heeled shoes. I follow her for a block or two before realizing that I've missed the next park entrance. Instead, I find myself outside of an accessories store. Though the glass has fogged up, the window displays are discernible. A row of silver jewelry rests neatly against a black velvet board. Next to the Muslim prayer hats and woolen slippers lies a silver tray with six matching cups. A colorful tapestry falls against one corner of the wall. I ring the doorbell and enter.

Sticks of cinnamon-colored incense burn in a small clay pot. A turquoise vase filled with dried flowers sits in the center of a round table. Around the vase, different types of hairpieces are displayed in a straw basket: head bands, ribbons, hats. Most of them are painted in various shades of white. As I play with the adornments, a woman in a blue sari brings out a box of scarves and veils.

"I haven't had a chance to put these out yet," she explains. I unfold a silk scarf and drape it over my head and neck. I experiment. I tie a knot on the side, but the look is too compliant. I tie a knot on the back and remember peasant girls roaming the rice fields in rolled-up pajama pants. No matter what I try, the scarf hangs limply from my neck. Maybe the pastel pinks and yellows are too mild for my temperament. Then I find a white embroidered veil with small black clovers sewn along its edges. Thin golden threads, woven into the fabric, sparkle under the store's fluorescent light like shooting stars speeding through the sky. I place the veil on my head.

My eyes fall upon an off-white dress hanging on the back wall of the store as I remove the veil. Antique lace borders its long sleeves and broad necklines and beige beads are sewed along the seams. I ask the woman if the dress belonged to someone. She nods. "It's not for sale. It belonged to my great grandmother," she explains, stroking the gown as if for the first time before giving it to me. I walk to the back wall of the store to feel the fabric. The owner climbs onto a ladder and lowers the dress for me.

"Are you looking for yourself?" the woman asks.

"No," I lie, "my sister."

Lying about my marriage comes more easily than telling the truth. There is so much to hide from people. When I confess that I'm engaged, they congratulate me and ask how Nicholas proposed. I tell them that Nicholas isn't the man I intend to marry, but Hamid, someone I know only slightly better than they do. "Just say 'no,'" my friends urge, as if Hamid were selling me drugs.

The woman shows me other dresses. "Maybe these will interest you," she says. I turn my head in the direction she is pointing, but I am not interested in anything else. I walk toward the body-length mirror near the cashier. I press the gown against my body and stare at my reflection in the mirror. I like the casual way the skirt drops to the floor like the descent of autumn leaves. Natural.

Uninflated. Probably this is the sort of wedding dress I'd be wearing if I were marrying for the right reasons.

Fatemeh

Every home has a distinctive odor. At Madar Joon's it was the essence of rosewater. At Yasaman's the stench of burnt leaves. At the Goshayeshes' it's the scent of bitter lemons. The walls, the tablecloth, the chairs. Everything emits a natural citric vapor that no air freshener could imitate.

"Some tea?" Hamid's mother asks, and I nod.

I don't know whether it's just me or whether her tea always lacks flavor, despite the wedges of lemon, sugar, and candy. As she refills my cup, Mrs. Goshayesh points to the large mirror and crystal candelabra—the traditional gifts accorded the bride by the groom's family. She tells me they're antique and we exchange stiff smiles. Then Mrs. Goshayesh takes a round pastry from the tray near me, and the scent of lemons grows stronger. She cuts the Danish and places the larger half in her mouth. When Hamid notices my stare, he says, "Please help yourself. We don't think of you as guests any more." To be polite, I reach out for a piece.

Finally, Hamid asks me about the *mahrieh,* the legal sum accorded to the bride in case of a divorce—the necessary but sometimes unpleasant ritual in Muslim weddings. I take my time before responding. Nasrin lowers her head. "Whatever you want," Hamid says, and the smell of bitter lemons grows stronger. I offer a symbolic sum—twelve gold coins in honor of the twelve Shi'i imams— and Hamid graciously accepts. Nasrin is relieved, too. Marriage, after all, is a contract, not just an affair of the heart. I know my daughter is not for sale, that she is priceless. Anyhow, our Islamic contracts are meaningless here. There are no guarantees for a happy marriage.

Injured Race Cars

Nasrin

A dried rose petal drops on the table. We sit in the smoking section of the restaurant even though Hamid requested nonsmoking seats. Every ten minutes or so, he glances at his watch or turns his head to see whether the waitress has brought the food. "Why are they so slow today?" he asks as a way of avoiding conversation with me. When the waitress eventually serves his broiled tuna, Hamid relaxes his brows, relieved to be eating instead of interacting. He discusses his food, yes, the fish is so fresh today. Do I like my food? "Yeah," I tell him, "I do." When we have exhausted the subject of food, I ask him about his day at the office.

"Tell me," I say, "what's going on with your Dallas project?"

"Lots," he says. "But I can't stay long. Is there a reason you wanted to meet?"

"Yes," I say.

"Do you need money?"

"No."

"What then?"

I pause for a minute.

"Just tell me," he says.

"I won't go through with it."

"What? Dallas?"

"No," I say. "The wedding."

By now, Hamid has stopped eating. He wipes his lips several times and drinks a full glass of water. "We were just engaged," he says, and I apologize for not confronting him earlier. Hamid avoids my eyes as best he can, but it's difficult because I'm staring at him. He opens his briefcase and pulls out a folder with yellow and green pieces of paper. He tells me that they are forms for him and me. When he has finished showing them to me, he places the folder back in his briefcase. As the waiter puts the check next to his half-full plate, he dismisses my comments, insisting that I will probably change my mind tomorrow.

"I won't," I say. "I'm sure."

"Why?" he asks.

I don't respond.

The church bells chime baroque choral music. I open my purse and place a jewelry box on the table as Hamid hands the waiter our check. Before Hamid has a chance to notice, I take my belongings and leave. I walk in large strides through the streets, seeking crowded corners and busy boulevards. When I reach Broadway, I look back just once to insure that no one has followed me to the office.

A truck lunges toward the traffic light but misses and hits the curb instead. A police officer rushes over to the truck driver to make sure he's okay. I enter my office building and wait by the elevator. A well-dressed man walks in behind me and we make casual conversation. The elevator takes longer than usual to make its way down. I decide to go across the street and buy a cup of coffee before returning to the office. The deli is located beneath some scaffolding. When I return, the man is still there. As we step into the elevator, he politely asks for my wallet. "What?" I ask, wondering if I've heard him correctly. He takes out a knife and repeats his question. "Here," I say. "Take it." As he grabs my wallet, he twists my arm with one hand. Then he forces his body on mine. When the elevator door opens, he darts outside. Someone chases him down the stairs, and another person approaches me and asks if I am okay. I don't know. I stare at the incongruous black-and-white tiles beneath my feet. As if a pawn on a chessboard, I imagine a series of moves on the tiles before walking out of the building.

Yasaman

Snowflakes drop from a gray sky, and a frail whiteness blankets the sidewalk. I leave a fresh trail in the snow as I pass the greengrocer, the post office, the florist. Footprints can reveal the unknowns about a person. The steep prints of the man in front of me, for instance, show a sense of mission. His gait flattens out only when he stops at the cash machine. But Ali's are elliptical like his drawings. Footprints alone could not divulge his secrets.

Injured Race Cars

I call his house but hang up when I recognize his voice. It's his tone, a deep sound darker than the blare of rusty trumpets. Ali has a day off from work. I will surprise him. Maybe we can spend it together doing something carefree, like ice skating. Or see the Matisse exhibition at the MOMA. Before reaching his apartment, I stop by a magazine store to pick up the recent issue of *Women's Wear Weekly*. I knock. There is no answer. I try once more. When no one responds, I take the key he gave me and open the door. Water boils in the kitchen, and steam moistens the room.

"Ali?"

I tiptoe toward the bedroom. The radio is on, and soft jazz tunes leak through the walls. When I open the bedroom door, the air inside is thick with human warmth. Two naked bodies lie entangled on blue sheets. Books and magazines surround them. They laugh softly. Ali caresses her hair and then notices me. I have never seen that naked woman before. Ali says something to me, but I can't understand. The bedroom sweat weakens my stomach, and I trip over two heavy raincoats as I leave the room. Weeping willows. I place the *Women's Wear Weekly* and his key on the coffee table and close the door behind me. A car honks loudly as I walk through a red light. I walk and walk until I reach the skating rink. The twirling skaters are no longer on the ice. In fact, I don't recognize anything on the streets, not even my footsteps. A fleeting rain has melted the snow, washing away its cryptic codes and shapes.

The candles are burning.

In the park, joggers warm the running trail near the skating rink A homeless man wraps himself in plastic bags to protect against the rain. Two skaters pirouette on the ice with outstretched hands. Their bodies spin out of control like injured race cars before colliding against the walls. As they position themselves again on the ice, bystanders applaud them, and they circle the rink several times before repeating their figures on the ice. What instinct forces people to rise up only to repeat the same mistakes?

I reach my apartment and rush to the bathroom. The water runs in the sink for a few seconds, and then I relieve myself. Before I turn off the faucet, there is a knock on the door. Nasrin calls my name. Then I hear Fereydun's voice. Even though I am not ready for them, they open the door and step inside. Sweat clings to my hair, and I feel hot. Nasrin approaches the sink and holds me tightly.

"I know," she says.

I am not sure what she knows.

Does she know about Ali?

The woman in his bed?

The blood that seeps out of my stomach?

"Please," she pleads. "Don't do this any more."

The candles are burning.

Fereydun wipes my mouth with a damp bathroom towel. As he leads me into the living room, I wait for the smell of burnt leaves to drift through the half-open window, but instead I smell fresh hyacinths. Nasrin hands me a card with a doctor's name and address. "If you want, I'll come with you," she says. Nasrin leaves the apartment to give us privacy. Fereydun and I sit on the couch and embrace each other without offering words. I rest my head on his body, although I know I will not fall asleep. He promises to stay with me. I want to run into the bathroom again, but my stomach constricts and I stop. I can hear the silence.

Fatemeh

Some memories have a limited time span. I can't remember a time when the three of us lived under one roof. It's the same for Muhsin. Yesterday he called, preoccupied about Nasrin. He sounded strangely out of sorts, insisting through his coughs that the *mahrieh* sum not be violated. Had Nasrin sent him photos of the engagement party? I didn't know and told him so. Did she like the engagement gift? he asked, referring to the gold earrings he'd ordered especially for the occasion. "Sure," I lied, even though I had no idea. Truth be told, I haven't seen her wear them once.

I didn't know how else to sate his curiosity. Fine, I said, fine. Eventually, Muhsin changed the subject.

Along Kissena Boulevard, a mosque sits on a neglected clod of land behind forsaken warehouses and dumpsters. I search for a large dome in a maze of brick buildings, but above my head I only find barren trees. I spot a group of veiled women on a seeming pilgrimage and follow them. They pause next to a shiny white building, and an old man with a turban emerges to greet them. I hadn't expected such simplicity in a mosque. There is no dome, just a two-dimensional cupola. Instead of turquoise tiles, the exterior is decorated with stucco. Bright red graffiti already defiles its walls. A boy sitting on a low stool paints over the "Fuck" with unstinting attention.

We enter a dark room with no windows. Women take their spots on the afghans arranged on the floor. A velvet curtain separates the women's quarters from the men's. As I prepare to begin the prayer, a woman notices my awkward movements and approaches with a glass of cold water. My hands shake as I take the glass from her. Instead of drinking it, I rub some on my face.

How do I tell Muhsin?

Rain drenches the cement. Kissena Boulevard stretches before us as I exit the mosque. The stench of dead fish and garlic signal the proximity of the local Korean market. The narrow street widens, as with one motion of a camera lens, to engirdle a large mass of honking cars. I can hear the greengrocers across the street exchanging anecdotes, or perhaps insults, in a patois unfamiliar to me. We're stuck in traffic.

When I return home, Nasrin opens the door. She strides across the room and hangs my coat in the bathroom. Then she sits down by the window and reads something called *California Caravan*. Sadness lingers around her lips when she smiles, but she does not discuss it. Some situations fail to force intimacy, and I do not press the matter. I just put a cup of tea beside her.

Hamid's mother called to tell me her son couldn't go through with it. She never let on that Nasrin had already called off the wedding. I practiced several times in front of the mirror before telling my husband. "Muhsin," I said to myself, "something has happened." Or "Muhsin, your daughter is upset." Finally, I said, "Muhsin, we've decided to cancel the wedding." He was silent for a few minutes. Then, he said, "Bring her back." For once, he spoke with conviction, with authority. He no longer questioned himself and I finally agreed with him, so I told him I would try.

"Come back," I tell Nasrin. "It's time."

Small sparkles fall out of Nasrin's eyes as she approaches me with an open embrace. She releases her hold on me and sits up straight on the bed. I don't insist. I sense a purpose guiding her decision, even though it may not be what I wish. The yearning to tarry overwhelms, but I step away. Somehow we survive from year to year, apart and yet together.

Faces of Parsa

Nasrin

Natives and tourists alike arrive in Iran with that same confounded stare. A gaze of exhaustion and curiosity after a twelve-hour stopover in Amsterdam followed by a six-hour flight. We've been in this state of uncertainty since entering Iranian air space. What will become of us once we're on the ground? Hours of questioning followed by a brief night in prison? Whipping? Or absolutely nothing? It's nearly impossible to predict. Expatriates traveling to and from Iran offer mixed reviews of the airport experience. Media reports from the old country are even more unreliable.

A customs official motions to me to move ahead in line. He looks almost identical to the other administrators boxed into the glass booths. A thick black moustache and an unfriendly tone of voice complete his austere appearance. Smiling is sanctioned by Islam though evidently not endorsed by the customs police. The frown has triumphed as the accepted form of public expression, since like the chador it conceals the individual behind a safe, contrived facade. So I have no qualms about wrinkling my brows as I approach the booth to present my passport.

"Why are you here?" he asks.

"To visit family," I say.

I keep my gaze down as the customs official takes my passport and reviews my entry forms. As I expect, in public, shaggy beards are the norm for men and the black hijab triumphs as the attire for women, but the beards and veils thinly disguise hidden desires and pleasures.

"What do you do in America?" he asks.

"I'm a translator," I say.

"Translating what? CIA transcripts?"

I laugh but stop quickly when I notice the officer's annoyance.

"Basic things, you know, birth certificates, death certificates, marriage certificates."

"So certificates," he concludes. "Is that all?"

"Pretty much," I say. "And instructions for electronic household items like coffee makers, food processors, that sort of thing."

Satisfied that I lead a boring and unthreatening existence in the land of the Great Satan, he stamps my passport and sends me to the baggage claim area, where after twenty minutes I retrieve my two suitcases and stand in line to have my luggage inspected.

"What's this?" a woman with thick white gloves asks as she removes my iPod, though I am quite certain she knows. She will likely impound it and repackage it as a present to her sons or nephews.

"It's for listening to music," I say.

"You can't bring this into the country," she says and confiscates it.

Finally, she sends me out to the airport lobby where cousins, aunts, and friends I haven't seen in years warmly greet me. One of them tells me I look thinner than my pictures; another that I should highlight my hair. It's three A.M. Tehran time—a customary arrival time for European flights to Iran. My family members are recognizable, too, despite the wrinkles acquired in the intervening years. My father walks in front of this crowd of relatives to greet me next. He coughs in my face before we kiss and embrace. Though the touch feels forced and alien, we smile through the experience. Porters looking for easy money circulate around my luggage. My father waves to one and leads him to the car. Before long, we're on the expressway back to a home I barely remember.

"Here's Martyrdom Street," he says, turning onto a boulevard lined with tulips and dried trees. "If you turn left and go straight," he manages in between coughs, "you'll still find your old elementary school."

I've lost my connection to Tehran as if it had never been a part of my life. The city's streets lead to unexpected places, to new mosques, schools, and cemeteries. The department stores are no longer lined up along the avenues in the order I'd remembered them. Neon lights flashing in bright shades of red and green advertise restaurants, pharmacies, and book stores I've never heard of before.

During all those months in America, Maman never warned me that Agha Jan was so ill. I don't ever remember him coughing incessantly into the telephone, barely able to carry on a conversation. How strange to think that a physiological function as natural as a cough is actually the sound of death slowly suffocating his body. When I mention the possibility of cancer, my mother changes the subject. Maman doesn't like to use the word as if by not uttering it she can wish his illness away.

"Agha Jan," I say, "have you been to the doctor lately?"

"What for?" he responds. "I'm fine." He smiles and hugs me tightly. "Really, don't worry about me," he manages, unable to stifle another deep cough. He turns his back to prevent me from seeing him breathe with effort. Agha Jan does not know any better. To him, I am still the twelve-year-old he had left behind more than a decade ago.

Fatemeh

A demonstrator outside Shah Abd al-Azim shrine washes his bloodied hands with rosewater. It is Ashura, the tenth of Muharram, and the anniversary of the death of the third Shi'i leader, Imam Husayn. Men march and beat their backs with iron chains to express their grief at the tragic death of Imam Husayn. Nasrin watches the rhythmic slap of the iron chains on bare flesh. The participants chant religious tunes as drummers beat their *dombaks* to the sounds of foreboding death.

Nasrin imbibes the scenery like a foreigner. On the outside, though, she looks like every other Iranian girl at the Ashura ceremony. Her hijab sits in place upon her head fastened by pins on both sides to prevent it from slipping off accidentally in public. She wears a long black manteau to blend in seamlessly with the other spectators. Her nails are short and unmanicured, and she refuses to wear makeup in public. In short, she sports the ideal image of the postrevolutionary woman.

"Won't all this blood on the pavement lead to a cholera outbreak or something?" Nasrin asks.

Perhaps, but that's not the point. She misses the intense spirituality of the experience—the steadfast faith of demonstrators, their identification with the fallen martyrs, their desire for remembrance of past injustices. These are the true bonds of religion. For Nasrin, though, these rituals are alien spectacles, events she never experienced as a youth in prerevolutionary Iran. Today, she stops by the street peddlers eager to buy worry beads and other religious paraphernalia as keepsakes of her trip back home. She opens a prayer book but can't make out the Arabic verses. There is no piety beyond her consumerism.

Nasrin

Zaynab, an old childhood friend, doesn't know I am visiting from the United States. I had tried calling her from New York before leaving. In Khanum Parvin's second-grade class, we became friends. She was wearing a purple bow in her thick black hair, most of which was hidden under a white headscarf. I didn't know any other child at the time who wore the veil. In fact, none of us at the Aryamehr School did. When Zaybab arrived, we weren't sure what to make of her. For days, we just stared. We stared as she colored her goldfish. We stared as she wrote the answers on the blackboard. We stared when she ate her greasy lunch of rice and *ghaymeh.* We listened intently as she read aloud the assigned stories in a heavy Isfahani accent.

One day, I forgot my lunch and Zaynab offered to share. At first, I didn't want to try her greasy *ghaymeh.* I was sure I'd grow a scarf on my head. But Khanum Parvin laughed when I told her why I wouldn't try the rice. She took a bite just to convince me that the rice had nothing to do with the headscarf. The day after, I brought Zaynab a Hershey bar that a relative had brought for me from America. She liked it. From the start, we were placed in the same reading group. Then we paired up for the annual Persian New Year play at school. She dressed up as the *seeb,* or apple, and I pranced around as the *seer,* or garlic.

Zaynab's father spent that year in prison, though we did not know it at the time. He worked at a mosque, and a coworker accused him of being involved with the Fedaiyan—the underground group of Islamist activists—but no one really knew for sure. Zaynab's family had explained away his absence as a business trip to Qum. Later, we learned he'd been tortured in the infamous Evin prison—his toenails were yanked out of his flesh and his feet dipped in boiling oil. When he was released, he limped and often talked to himself. Not long after, he discovered opium. At night, he would lay out a kelim on the patio of his family home. There, he would light his small coal cooker and skewer tiny bits of opium on the fire. When my mother came to pick me up, she saw the opium. I was not allowed to have a playdate at their home again.

Zaynab is now a married woman, wife of a midlevel government official she'd met at Tehran University and a political candidate for the parliamentary elections. She will never let on that she and her husband had been friendly before the wedding.

I dial Zaynab's house again.

In elementary school, Zaynab and I had declared each other best friends. It's been about ten years since I've seen her, though I can still remember her parent's home number: 725-1148. There's no point in leaving a message for Zaynab. Who knows, I may not even have the right number. I think of other people from my childhood I might want to call, but there's no telling if they're still living in Iran. We've been dispersed like pollen across alien lands. On the third try, Zaynab picks up the phone—her voice still guttural and fierce. She can't talk for long since she's on her way to a campaign stop in the province of Mazandaran, where the farmers have embraced her promises of land reform. Her face, though barely exposed to the camera, is plastered on the covers of two magazines, as reminders that women are participants in the electoral process, too.

"The driver can swing by so I can see you for a few minutes," she suggests.

I consent.

Zaynab arrives with some Persian pastries purchased at a bakery near her home. Zaynab smells of rosewater, body odor, and Chanel No. 5 all at once. She's put on weight, too. She talks about her husband, his contacts, and all the perks that come with his government appointment.

"You remember, before the revolution we didn't own a car. Not even a motorcycle."

I nod.

"Now I'm paralyzed without the car, the driver, the cook," she laughs, fixing her *maqna'ah.*

"How did you meet?" I ask.

She smiles. "C'mon," she prods, "you know I come from a religious family. Anyway, he's a second cousin on my mother's side." Before I can respond, she adds, "I hear it's worse in the United States where first cousins regularly marry each other. Is that true?"

"I don't know," I say, though this very well may be the case. "They do have same-sex marriages," I add with a grin.

Zaynab asks about my life in America, my intention to marry, whether I dye my hair, and my salary. Quite abruptly she interrupts me and blurts out, "So why have you come back?" She asks the question as if to say that the country no longer belongs to the likes of me.

I am not sure and tell her so.

She seems unconvinced and adds with an insincere laugh, "Has the CIA sent you here on a covert operation?" But feeling guilty for her lack of friendliness, she tries to redeem herself and asks instead about my father's deteriorating health.

"My uncle died of lung cancer," she recalls.

"I'm sorry," I offer but don't really want to hear more about the subject.

"When things got really bad, my aunt hired a nurse so they could administer the morphine at home."

Zaynab senses my anxiety and changes the subject.

"Where are you headed?" I ask, expecting a convenient fib for a reply.

To my chagrin, she answers honestly. "A girls' elementary school in Shimiran," she says. "Want to come along?"

"What's there?"

"I'm supposed to meet young girls and encourage them to be good mothers and wives, even as they campaign for a political seat. They want me to participate in the school prayer as well."

I laugh. "You never used to pray when you were their age."

She nods. "But they don't know that," she confides.

Zaynab keeps up the pretense to satisfy her children, her husband, her constituency, and her country—if not her conscience.

"Do you want to come along?"

I shake my head. We both know I would be considered a campaign liability.

After a week in Tehran, it becomes apparent that satellite television is the most popular form of domestic entertainment here. TV access is also a bellwether of political currents in the country. During a downturn, the satellite dishes disappear from view. They reappear with news about rising inflation and unemployment. We are now experiencing an interval of media accessibility, though public prayers and religious talk shows dominate the television broadcasts. On the evening news, there's no mention of the sporadic riots in Mazandaran province, where Zaynab will be campaigning.

Luckily, my cousin Kimiya drops by uninvited. Like me, she'd left after the revolution but returned to Iran from France three years earlier to start a business as a jewelry designer. She decides to take me to an Internet café for breakfast. I am at once thrilled and embarrassed for wanting to partake of this completely touristy experience. She drives us to a café run by her former college roommate. We order a cappuccino and try to Google some of our favorite sites, like Youtube and Facebook, but discover that censors have blocked those Web pages.

"You can still check your email," she volunteers.

"Nah," I say. "On my vacation."

We pay and plan the rest of the day. "I'll show you around," Kimiya says as we leave the Internet café. On the street, we run into Agha Reza, my building janitor qua neighborhood watchdog. He talks to me about the plumbing problems in the basement and watches intently as I climb into Kimiya's car. When we reach the intersection of Independence Avenue and Martyrdom Street, Kimiya asks matter-of-factly, "Are you still a virgin?"

Huh? Where did this come from? After all, we hadn't spoken to each other with such candor for years. Shouldn't there be a gradual icebreaker before we plunge into the personal dirt accumulated over fourteen years of separation? Although stunned by her directness, I feign composure and reply, "Of course. Aren't we all?"

She laughs. "I'm not," she admits. "Haven't been for years." She watches my face for a reaction. "Come on," she taunts. "I spent my teenage years in Paris."

"People always lie about sex, one way or another."

"Are you?" she asks, suspecting more beneath my cool demeanor.

"I never did it with Hamid," I say.

"You know the rumors, though."

I nod. The scuttlebutt was that we did it and he broke off the engagement. "It was perpetuated by his mother. Whatever."

"I did it with a French guy when I was sixteen," she goes on. "I'd never do it with an Iranian, though," she confesses.

"Why?" I ask.

"Could you imagine—hairy, selfish, overeager."

We laugh.

"Not to mention all the gossip. Just look at Yasamin."

"What do you mean?" I probe.

"You know, Yasaman and that divorced guy, Ali."

"Hadn't heard," I lie, though she probably detects my disingenuousness.

"What does it matter in the end? You can be a virgin and then after a few years your husband can take another wife without your knowledge. Either way, it sucks for us. "

"Not if you have money," I say. "Look at you—with your own jewelry business now. Can I see your store?"

"Sure. We can drive by later." Then she points out the window and says, "Hey look! There's your baby brother."

I don't know what she is talking about. "My baby brother? What do you mean?"

She's silent. "Oh geez," she blurts out. "You have no idea."

"I thought my mom went through menopause."

She parks the car and we walk to her jewelry shop. Her designs eschew the traditional gilded techniques of Iranian craftsmen. Instead, she combines post-modern sensibility with classic Persian artistry. Gemstones like amber and lapis lazuli are set off with pearls and diamonds in antique silver frames.

"Here, try this on," she says without waiting for a reply. She fastens an amethyst pendant with a black braided cord around my neck.

"I love it," I say and mean it.

Her assistant places it in a floral trinket box and offers it to me as a gift.

"Don't ta'rof please," she insists as I prepare to protest. "Just enjoy it."

"Thanks," I say, taking the pendant out of the box and putting it around my neck.

We leave the store and walk a few blocks to a pizza joint. Kimiya orders a mushroom and onion pizza just like we might have done in London or New York. The only difference here is that we're fully covered from head to toe, and the unaccompanied girls sit at separate tables from the boys. The girls have succumbed to teenage Islamic fashion, sporting bright colorful headscarves and short petticoats ironically known by a French word, manteau. They stare at us, dressed as we are in bland colors like beige and navy. Amidst these stares, Kimiya tells me about my father's "other" wife.

"Is she pretty?" I ask. "Smart? Young?" What could this woman possibly offer my father that my mother did not?

"I don't know," she says.

What exactly is this woman to me? She is obviously not my mother, not an aunt, not a mother-in-law. At last, I understand the silence between my mother and father. Their strained conversations. The emptiness of their embrace.

"What's my brother's name?"

Kimiya can't remember.

Kimiya lives in a one-bedroom just below her parents' apartment. We go through a dark and dingy lobby with large mirrors nailed on stained gray walls. Hers is the last one to the left of the stairway. She opens the door slowly, and a wrinkle-faced dog juts his head out, wagging his tail wildly with delight. I think he smells food. I am fascinated by her apartment, which resembles a local family-run antique shop, except that none of the objects she's assembled is valuable. There's her sitar in one corner and a guitar in another.

"Whose is this?" I ask, referring to the sitar.

"Mine. I took lessons a few years ago."

On the mantelpiece there's a jar filled with strands of hair. I turn the jar carefully to figure out why she's placed them here.

"That's my lineage," Kimiya explains as if reading my mind. "At least as far back as four generations ago."

How can she tell which strand of hair belongs to whom? Maybe it doesn't matter. But I eventually drive myself crazy wondering, so I ask her.

"It's all in the texture and color," she explains. "If the colors are the same, I can tell from the thickness and the type, who it belongs to." She takes the jar from my hand and opens the lid. "This one belongs to my uncle Sepehr," she says, gently disentangling it from the others. She is really very involved with her collection, an odd hobby she's acquired since the revolution.

Her bedroom walls are decorated with old calendar pages. She keeps the extras in a suitcase under her bed. I ask her why she has so many. "It makes me feel like I've been alive a lot longer than I really have," she explains. I think I must have given her a wry smile because she adds, "Just imagine how long two thousand days might be." I try, but it's beyond me. Everything she owns has a story. Not at all like my place, where it's impossible to trace anything very far into the past.

"Do you think there's going to be a war?" she asks.

"Yes."

"Why?"

"Because there's unfinished business."

"Whose business? Israel's? Iran's? America's?"

I don't know. It doesn't matter anyhow whose business it is. When hatred guides political decisions, what good can come of it?

A motorcyclist swerves off the road and hits an old Toyota. Other cars stall in the middle lane of the expressway. Frustrated, drivers honk their horns without interruption, waiting for the police to arrive. We are caught in Tehran's infamous traffic, just blocks away from the university. An hour later, when we finally extricate ourselves from the jam, Kimiya parks the car and enters the campus, the site of so many political rallies and shattered dreams. Today, the university is quiet. No student riots or Friday prayers. Kimiya takes me to the membership office so I can get a visitor's pass. A long line has formed in the hallway, since the manager is still at lunch at 2:30 P.M. The office closes at 4:00. Young men and women utter complaints and obscenities to themselves. They speak loud enough to be heard by the bystanders in line, but not by the office staff. Finally, a short man with a thick black mustache and a brown polyester suit appears. He calls people into his office one by one. As Kimiya and I approach his desk, we're interrupted by a skirmish in the hallway.

"What's going on?" the clerk demands.

A male university student was barred from entering the library and arrested by the university police. "He's the cartoonist for the student newspaper," someone whispers. In the last issue of the satirical journal *Nakhandi* (Don't Laugh), he published a caricature of the Supreme Leader wearing an Elvis suit and listening to rock-and-roll music, instead of the anticipated *rowzeh khani* prayers, with his flashy iPod.

"Am I going to Evin?" the cartoonist asks with a wry smile, referring to the prison in northern Tehran where dissidents spend time reconsidering their political proclivities.

"Shut up," the policeman says, hitting him in the rib with a baton and handcuffing him. The cartoonist glares with contempt but then guffaws uncontrollably, yelling *"nakhandi, nakhandi"* as the policeman drags him into the patrol car. The office is quiet again, except for the voice of the clerk, who finally summons me to his desk.

"Where do you live in America?" he asks.

"New York City," I say.

"Wait here," he requests. He moves through the line, quickly approving permits and when the last person leaves, he tells me to approach his desk once again. "Here's your permit," he offers, handing me my slip with a note clipped to it. "It's good for a month." As I leave the office, I open the note and find the clerk's name—Hossein—along with his cell phone number written down.

"Does he really think I'm going to call him?" I ask Kimiya.

"Who knows. Maybe he's testing you. Just pretend it never happened," she advises as we head to the library. There, we quickly learn from the network of gossiping librarians that the cartoonist has been sent to Evin prison. Someone will likely contact his family, and the long wait for his release—dead or alive—will begin.

Still, I am impressed with the clerk's inventiveness. Given all the scrutiny over male-female relations, how is it that abortions, premarital sex, AIDS, and drug abuse proliferate throughout the country? Kimiya explains it to me. "There's no other entertainment. Don't forget our temporary marriages, either," she goes on. "Prostitution made legal and guilt-free."

We laugh.

"Anyhow, the guards can't report every sinner," she continues. "Only the rich and *'taghooti* monarchist types because they're willing to pay to get their kids out of trouble."

But it's hard to believe that every guard lacks conviction or is freed from the burdens of his ethics and personal judgments. As we leave the university grounds, Kimiya writhes over in pain and holds her left hip.

"What is it?" I ask.

"Can you drive the car back to my place?"

"I don't have a license."

"Please, you have to," she pleads.

"Okay," I say.

"Just drive me home. I'll tell you where to go."

"Do you need to go to a doctor?"

"No. I'm all right. I get these pains from time to time."

Faces of Parsa

I drive the car like an elderly person who is sitting behind the wheel for the first time. Tentative, confused, and scared of everything in sight that moves and has wheels, I still manage to reach the northern outskirts of the capital. Although it is not the norm in Tehran, I respect the traffic rules: I stop at red lights, stay in my lane, and stick to the speed limit. Before long, people roll down their windows and yell obscenities at me. "Where did you learn to drive?" someone demands. "In the provinces?" He quickly speeds by.

As we go past the Imam's mausoleum, Kimiya tells me about how she had dated her sitar teacher, Ahmad. She'd have the lessons at her parents' apartment so as not to arouse the suspicion of neighbors. Kimiya picked up the sitar quickly, having played the guitar for years.

"One day I discovered I was pregnant," she continues.

"I'm sorry," I say, guessing the outcome.

"It wasn't easy, you know." She stops.

"Did you tell your mom?" I ask.

She shakes her head. At first, Kimiya went to Zaynab, hoping Zaynab could recommend a doctor the government couldn't track. Zaynab panicked, but her uncle gave Kimiya the name of someone who did abortions in his office. Sometimes men are better in crisis situations specific to women.

"Then I got sick. An infection, bleeding that wouldn't end. So my father sent me to Paris."

"Did the guy know?"

"No. I never told him. Ahmad had two kids, an opium habit, a bad marriage. There was no point to it." Kimiya still lives with the ghosts of that relationship as her body succumbs to these cramps and bleeding spells.

Fatemeh

This is probably not a good idea. I have for years resisted the temptation to come to Afsaneh's corner of Tehran. The cheap smell of lamb kebobs fills the long boulevard that eventually turns into her quarter of the city. Peasant boys stand behind the portable carts along the sidewalk. One of them pulls out corn husks with vigor and fans the grilled ears before dipping them in saltwater and giving them to customers. I ask Nasrin if she'd like to try one but she declines. She is anxious to meet Afsaneh and her half-brother.

"Why didn't you tell me?" she asks again.

"I couldn't," I answer.

What was there to say, that perhaps we should have divorced? The dishonor of divorce seemed preferable to the humiliation of bigamy.

As we approach Afsaneh's apartment building, my crippled hand quivers and the corn falls in the *jube,* the irrigation canals that border Tehran's streets.

"Maman," Nasrin offers, "you don't have to come with me."

I nod.

"I need to meet them, though," she explains.

I don't really understand but refrain from telling her so.

The meeting might actually give her an explanation for Muhsin's actions, a justification that I can't possibly provide.

Nasrin

Iranian flags drape the cars heading to Azadi Stadium. From a distance, it seems as if the city is dyed in the tricolors of green, white, and red. Tehran prepares itself for the final qualifying match of the World Cup between Iran and Australia. We join in the commotion that has erupted in the streets.

"I met them," I whisper to Kimiya in the backseat of Keyvan's antiquated Honda.

"Who?" she asks.

"The other woman."

"And?"

"I don't think she liked me," I confess.

"Let it go," she advises.

"What are you two gossiping about?" our cousin Keyvan probes, feigning annoyance.

Kimiya changes the subject. Women are technically barred from soccer matches, so we made plans to watch the game on TV at Keyvan's home with some friends.

Although I would have liked to sneak into the soccer match, Keyvan warned against it. The truth is, I've never been to a sporting event in Iran. My parents eschewed modern sports like soccer and tennis, considering them a waste of time and foreign imports. Nowadays, competition is restricted for women, which suits me just fine. I prefer channeling my energies into spectator sports, usually in the comfort and security of the living room.

Keyvan's friends arrive one by one with unexpected goodies in hand: beer and wine. The illicit alcohol is cleverly hidden in diaper bags and beneath baby blankets. We catch parts of the game on BBC World News. A scare on our end followed by one for the Australian goalie. Then, almost unexpectedly, the Australian forward dribbles past the Iranian fullbacks and heads the ball into the net. The stadium—and Keyvan's apartment—erupts in a collective cry of despair. Australia wins the game 2-1.

Kimiya opens the balcony window. Isolated gunshots reverberate in the distance. People representing different ends of the political spectrum shout random slogans in the streets. Outside, a group of thirty women bedecked with headscarves in the colors of the flag shout slogans—"long live Iran." A police officer blows his whistle to disperse them. Then a group of angry spectators throws pumpkin seeds at the guards and a scuffle ensues.

"Do you smell that?" Kimiya asks, referring to an acidic odor in the air.

I nod.

"It's tear gas," she says, dragging me to the balcony.

"I can't breathe," I say feeling slightly panicked. "Shut the window!"

"Don't worry," Kimiya laughs. "It'll pass."

We leave the balcony door ajar and step inside the living room. Keyvan grabs his wallet from the table to pay the pizza delivery boy. As he steps into the hallway, the delivery boy walks toward Keyvan's apartment with two other men flanking him on either side.

"Shit," Keyvan mutters to himself. He quickly shuts the door and warns everyone to hide the alcoholic drinks as quickly as possible. The men in the apartment try to get rid of the alcohol, while the women search for their headscarves.

When the delivery boy reaches the door, Keyvan gives him a stack of 1,000 toman bills. But his buddies don't seem satisfied with the cash.

"I smell liquor," one of the Komiteh guards says.

Keyvan's friend intervenes and offers more cash.

"Are the girls relatives of yours?"

"Of course," Kimiya says taking out her national ID card to show it to the officer.

"What about the rest of you?"

"They're relatives," Keyvan asserts. "Now go."

Keyvan, Kimiya, and I follow the men to the lobby. There, the guards join other Komiteh officers who had apparently searched several units in Keyvan's apartment complex. Two girls and a boy have been arrested by the Komiteh guards. The arresting officer, a boy not much older than the youth he's detained, tells his partner that the girls should be subjected to a virginity test at the local precinct.

"What happens if she's not a virgin?" I ask Keyvan.

"I'm not sure. She could be whipped," Keyvan answers, "but they do it gently. No one wants to earn a reputation as a butcher of young girls."

"And her family?" I ask.

"They can pay for surgery to re-virginize her."

How does Keyvan know this?

"Have you ever . . ."

He lifts up his shirt to show three stray scars across his ribcage. Even the fear of corporal punishment doesn't prevent the youth from risking the natural acts of intimacy. I have countless other questions about the business of re-virginization. Who does the surgery? How long is the recovery? Keyvan doesn't know.

Fatemeh

Muhsin stands by the edge of the sea, motionless. He smokes his cigar and watches the waves crest and crash against a rock, breathing heavily in between screeching coughs. The last vacation Muhsin and I spent along the Caspian shore was at an isolated cottage with little running water. We were staying at a summer home that belonged to one of his distant relatives. With Nasrin here, we decided to get away from the city and come here again. On the first day, Muhsin and I created a comfortable routine: breakfast, reading, backgammon, lunch, beach, relatives, and sleep. When we weren't sticking to the routine, we fought. About little things. About big things, too, but always behind Nasrin's back. When Nasrin was around, we worked hard to make our lives appear normal, familial. As soon as she went out with her friends, we stopped pretending. Muhsin was getting weaker by the day.

"Where's Nasrin?" Muhsin asks.

"Out with Kimiya," I say.

"Nasrin doesn't like spending any time with us," Muhsin complains. "She's used to not having us around."

"I don't think it's that." I say.

The truth is, we hadn't prepared Nasrin for Muhsin's condition. He had taken a turn for the worse, with the cancer spreading to his liver and colon. Even I didn't know about his deteriorating health until after my return from America. He and Afsaneh had decided together not to pursue any treatments. "What the use?" Muhsin had reasoned. They'd convinced themselves that his time had come.

I offer him some tea and sour cherry jam. Just then, Muhsin's other wife calls to speak to him about something "urgent." "Sure," I say, deferential, handing him the phone. She's the only woman, other than me, who has been in a long-term relationship with Muhsin. In fact, for many years, though I don't know the actual number. I pass the receiver and walk into the kitchen. As I read the morning paper, I wait for Muhsin to finish his talk with Afsaneh. When Muhsin hangs up the phone, I pretend not to care about his "urgent" telephone conversation, though I desperately want to know.

"Did your test results arrive?" I ask.

He shrugs his shoulders and leaves the cottage without offering an answer. What a mess he has made of our lives. When he goes, there will be the inevitable arguments over inheritance, the rights of Nasrin and Nezam, Afsaneh's son and Muhsin's four-year-old male heir. Who will live in our home?

I search through Muhsin's briefcase for a copy of his will, for any clues about his other life. I even dial the phone to speak to Afsaneh—actually, to scream and yell at her for the intrusion into my world. But before I press the last number, I hang up. They have long known that I am too weak to confront them. This is probably why Muhsin listens to her and not to me.

I find a slip of paper with an address in the side pocket of his briefcase. The place is just a couple of kilometers from where we're staying, so I drive over. There are no signs of current occupancy at the dilapidated shed. I open the door and walk through a living room furnished with dusty chairs and tables. A small charcoal grill burns morsels of opium.

"Fatemeh?"

I walk toward the voice and find Muhsin sitting on an old wooden chair looking outside the broken kitchen window. A mild breeze floats through the cracked glass, saturating the room with the scent of burning opium. He hands me a rusted iron chain. When we had first gotten married, Muhsin and I walked past this cottage and we'd found it. A memento, he'd said, that would bind us together, once in joy, now in silence.

"I knew you'd come," he confesses. "Forgive me."

What does forgiveness mean at the moment of death? In his weakness, Muhsin no longer questions my God. His lungs have filled with fluid, and his body shakes with every exertion. He tugs at the iron chain heaving to breathe. Muhsin touches my hand and we embrace, a union as laden with tenderness as with sorrow. I twist the aged iron chain around our bodies and feel the weight of Muhsin's arms before he collapses to the ground.

Nasrin

The haunting scent of a dead man's cologne imbues my parents' bedroom. Maman has not disturbed the décor. He went quickly, she said. Peacefully. How serene could it really have been if he was heaving for every breath? Without morphine? Or oxygen? Still conscious of his illness and the limitations of his deteriorating body?

Women shrouded in black enter through the curtain and claim seats. Kimiya takes the tray of dates and offers them to the well-wishers, many of whom I do not even know, friends and acquaintances my parents amassed during my years of absence from their lives. Male relatives trickle into the gilded mosque through a separate entrance on Martyrdom Street to listen to Hajj Agha pay homage to my father. He recites doleful verses, first in Persian then in Arabic. Final prayers. The summation of a life's worth.

A large black-and-white picture of my father from his youth is placed on a mantelpiece before the *mambar* for all to see. He is wearing casual clothes and stands in the cobblestone yard of his family home in Rasht. Once the city of their dreams, Rasht was where my mother and father had met, fallen in love, and gotten married. They settled on raising a small family, the sort an academic could afford, consisting of a mother, a father, and a kid. My parents were an average middle-class couple with few expectations. Happy to lead a simple, uneventful life, they filled their days with things that came most naturally to them like working, cooking, or contemplating. They moved to Tehran sometime after I was born. The city was experiencing an economic boom at the time. Oil money was filtering in. My father even had a brief stint working as an engineering consultant for the oil company. But they had not expected the intrusion of politics into their lives.

Afraid to rupture the stasis, my parents had trained themselves to accept with reserve the pains and joys of life. A broken ankle, a promotion, they approached every aberration from our daily routine with the same guarded sensibility. Even my father's death happened as a natural part of the cycle of life, like a serene winter snowfall or the blossoming of spring roses. He had been a smoker, so it came as little surprise when the doctors discovered his lung cancer. His death, like my birth, had been anticipated.

My half-brother rocks himself to sleep on my lap. Afsaneh watches us and smiles. Today she does not feel the urge to shelter him from us, his "other" family. Nezam will never know our father though he has inherited Agha Jan's long forehead and green eyes. What shall I tell him about Agha Jan when he is old enough to ask? That our dad was a scholar, a victim of politics, a coward? Maybe I will tell him nothing. He might find the unknown to be liberating, to imagine our father in any way he pleases.

When Hajj Agha finishes his sermon, we leave the mosque and stand next to the post office on Martyrdom Street. A man sorts through random letters written by mothers, convicts, and lovers. From my purse, I retrieve an envelope that arrived days earlier, a letter composed only of bars of musical notes. When I sound them out in my head, I hear Mendelssohn's violin concerto. Maybe, I think. Maybe Nicholas knows. But what is passion without words?

Military jets circle the skies above us. Hamid steps outside the mosque with the other male mourners. His hair is no longer glued together stiff with gel, though he's still impeccably dressed in a tailored suit. He approaches with a sullen expression as soon as he recognizes me.

"I've been here for a month," he explains. "I'm sorry," he offers.

"Thanks for coming," I say.

He lowers his head.

"Have you moved to Dallas yet?" I ask him.

"No."

"Oh?"

"I'll be taking over my father's business," he admits. Hamid's father had built a lucrative paper factory in Iran and Dubai after the war. They owned a virtual monopoly on the market, supplying tissues, diapers, and notebooks to consumers, stores, and schools in the region. The company was headquartered in Shiraz and closed for a few years after the revolution. But business resumed once the war ended. Hamid had for a time refused to enter his father's line of work, occupying himself instead with starting his private engineering consulting firm in New York, Los Angeles, and then Dallas.

"Does that mean you'll be living in Shiraz?" I ask.

"No, Dubai. I'll be traveling back and forth."

He is not wearing a ring. I look for clues about his personal life. In fact, I want to ask him so many questions, but there is no time. Mourners interrupt us to offer their condolences. Without saying good-bye, Hamid moves away.

"Nasrin, Nasrin, Naaaasrin . . ."

What?

Fatemeh

Nasrin has escaped death but she can't sense it yet. Maybe the realization will hit her months, even years, later in unlikely places—at an outing, in a restaurant, at work. Silence envelops the room. The only noise comes from the antiquated medical equipment in the hospital and the blood pressure machine that needs gentle prodding before it registers a number. Two nurses wearing pristine white veils and robes hover by her bedside. I play with my prayer beads as they adjust the IV bag with saline solution and antibiotics. With my thumb I flick the worry beads from one end to the next. I can even fiddle with it using my injured hand, but I quickly put the *tasbih* away when one of the nurses smiles at me with approval.

"Maman?"

"I'm here," I say.

She gropes for my hand.

Hamid had rushed her here. I heard him call out her name again and again to watch out for the van. It struck her and moved on without slowing. When they arrived at the hospital, there was only one young emergency doctor on duty. Somehow she managed to save Nasrin's life. She is now "in stable condition," though she hardly looks it with a damaged spleen and bruises on her face.

"Fatemeh, go home," Shirin says. "I'll spend the night with Nasrin."

I shake my head.

Shirin insists. She loves Nasrin insofar as another woman can truly love someone else's child. But Nasrin doesn't remember her well. Shirin became a recluse once she and her husband resolved not to have kids. Shirin got tired of watching her childhood friends become pregnant and share with pride stories of their children's milestones, birthday parties, and perfect report cards. Instead, Shirin lavished attention on herself by having cosmetic surgery. Anything to preserve her fleeting fame as a beauty pageant winner until her husband passed. Then she no longer felt the urge to stay youthful. Maybe she just came to terms with her age or maybe the anger in her quietly extinguished with the man's departure. When Shirin inherited her husband's money, she founded a tiny orphanage in Rasht and kept it so quiet that I only learned about it on my last trip there.

Shirin holds Nasrin's hand as she rests. She smiles when Hamid enters the room with a bouquet of lilies in a delicate glass vase. He sets it on the movable table near her bed. Hamid reaches over Nasrin for a moment, maybe to touch her face but stops when he sees us looking at him. He knows better than to give her a kiss in this state-run hospital.

"Did she wake up?" he asks.

I nod. "She's still heavily drugged."

"I'm glad," he says with gentleness. Hamid volunteers to spend the night at the hospital, even though his offer is merely a gesture of *ta'rof.* He assures me that he will visit frequently until she is out of the hospital. But we both know his mother would not want him near Nasrin. Not now. She would consider Nasrin a bad omen, *"bad ghadam,"* someone whose approach signals foreboding.

"Did they say when that might be?" he asks.

I shake my head. What does it matter really, today, tomorrow, or next week? Her physical injuries will heal in time, however imperfectly. The emotional ones will become her life's burden.

Nasrin

Sheets of paper in washed-out shades of red and yellow crack at the lightest human touch. Only the printed propaganda in the middle of the page retains its form. Weighty words like justice and freedom in bolded and enlarged letters fill the page. Words intended to prey on teenage innocence and to send them in quest of lofty ideals where instead they'll find their untimely deaths by guns and rifles. This stack of political flyers, once distributed daily in school, has now lost its vitality. When I walk through the city, I rely on these memories to guide me through old neighborhoods. Instead of flyers, political graffiti on the exterior of Tehran's buildings offer paeans to martyrs and broadcast revolutionary messages about veiling and the Great Satan. Eventually, I get lost in the maze of modern apartment buildings, expressways, and artwork that never existed in my childhood.

"Where is Shah Reza Avenue?" I ask a bystander.

He looks young, aggrieved, no doubt the progeny of the revolution, with his white polyester shirt yellowed around the collar and unbuttoned.

"Huh?" he responds.

"I mean, Martyrdom Street," I correct myself.

He points to a boulevard and sends me on my way.

I approach my old school and wait outside of the wide green gate that still opens promptly at eight every morning to let the students through. Veiled teenage girls search for salvation by reciting the Qur'an en masse in the courtyard instead of seeking divinity in Sufi poetry. It was at this site where girls and boys, Americans and Iranians, Jews and Muslims, once sat in class together and shared snacks during recess. It was here that young demagogues would greet their fans and distribute censored cassettes about social justice and rebellion. It was here, in one of those immured classrooms on the second floor, that the soldier found me leafing through the poetry collection. A room emptied of chairs, desks, and unbridled thoughts.

At the kiosk next to the gate, someone leads me to a small area cordoned off by a black curtain. The female guard takes my hands and looks at my nails. They are unpainted, unmanicured, but still apparently too long. She asks me to take off my shoes. My nylons too thin and light. Then she asks for my identification card. I try to offer something appropriate—a passport, a national card, a husband. No, says the female guard, no. These will not do. I cannot enter the school.

☙

An indifferent sun fades beneath a scarlet horizon. The sky changes colors assuming multiple personas, first enflaming the clouds with shades of orange and ginger before settling into a cool sapphirine blue. Nighttime arrives again on schedule. Sometimes, for diversion, Maman invites her special evening guests, mostly widows like herself who look back with reserve at what their lives might have been now that their husbands are gone and their children all grown up.

Tonight, it is Maman's turn to visit Shirin. But she will surely return by midnight to take her pills. Maman stresses that the medication eases the constriction in her hands, but we both know that it is really the intangible pains she strives to suppress—the disappointments of her marriage and her unspoken disenchantment of me—sorrows that resist measurement.

My restlessness peaks at dusk with each new cycle of darkness. I walk to the kitchen window and look outside, where the alley prostrates itself before the dilapidated homes of this once prosperous neighborhood. At one point, our district was considered up and coming, a *quartier* in which young couples willingly invested. They experimented with new architectural forms, townhouses with large garages that seemed strangely out of place next to the stylized old homes made of mud or brick and ornamented with gilded tiles and stucco. Modern homes burgeoned along the side streets as quickly as the unions that brought these young owners and their children to our streets.

But the neighborhood's development became stunted. Plans to build a gas station and a food court never came to fruition. Pedestrians traipsing down the alley to the corner store can still glimpse the broken bricks and stones as inchoate remnants of the abandoned construction. Although the overall price of Tehran real estate increased exponentially during the intervening years, the homes in this district have barely kept their value. Whatever became of their promise?

Fatemeh

The radio crackles like an old man clearing his throat. Eventually it clears, airing the voice of an Iranian newscaster. At two A.M. a news and information program run by Iranian emigrés is broadcast on WXIL. This is the only time I can follow the feature story without missing a point. Iranian businessmen in Los Angeles finance most of the program with their advertisements, which take up at least a third of the air time. I listen to world news for a while. There's a story about a drug dealer arrested in Japan, another about the parliamentary elections in Iran, and then more commercials.

Martyrdom Street

Nasrin wanders through the house repelling sleep. For months after her school shut down, she suffered from insomnia. On the night of the revolution when the sound of tankers outside the streets kept the neighborhood awake, Nasrin's tiny body quivered with the echo of every bullet that went off in the distance. The fear of unsightly violence confined her to the house. For days, Nasrin refused to leave her bedroom. The haggling in the bazaar, the gaze of strangers, even the deserted cars in the neighborhood frightened her months after the bullets had ceased reverberating in the streets. Sometimes she would sit in the garden holding Madar Joon's cane to ward off invisible enemies. But at night, she could not fall asleep.

Her imprisonment ended when we found her a new school. An Islamic school that imposed a bland grey uniform—a *rupush*—and a black veil. A school that forbade her from wearing skirts and painting her nails. Even with all its restrictions, the Islamic school restored her childhood, a right politics had seized. She gossiped about her teachers and invited friends to the house, though she knew never to discuss politics with them. For a time she even stopped talking in her sleep.

But innocence does not last long. One day, Nasrin returned home with a flier in her hand. Revolutionary slogans were printed in small letters on colored sheets of paper. "Neither East nor West! Death to the Shah! Long Live the Islamic Republic!" Beneath the slogans, Muhsin found the purpose of the revolution: "Embrace the Party of God!" Angry, Muhsin grabbed the flier out of her hand and ripped it into shreds. "Lies," he yelled, "lies." This was no way to educate the youth.

Muhsin decided then to send her abroad. I opposed the idea. She would do well enough here, speaking our language and living close to home. "Give it time," I said. "The country has to rebuild." The Pahlavi schools functioned worse, I reminded him, with their intermingling of sexes. But Muhsin was adamant. "If we don't send her out, they will poison her mind." In the following weeks, Muhsin struggled to find Nasrin an alternative. He planned a lifetime with his good friend, Reza Behmanesh, whose daughter Yasaman fared no better in the Islamic schools. Together they reasoned that our daughters would find happiness far from here, away from the duplicity of revolutionaries. What about the schools there? I said. The drugs? The sex? Who would look after her? It was only a temporary arrangement, he assured me. But temporary turned into eternity.

Faces of Parsa

Nasrin

Rain pounds the pavement. Streaks of water trickle down the window, and droplets of rain drip into a tin can from the kitchen ceiling. Our home is in desperate need of repairs. Black blotches discolor the wooden flooring, and paint chips off the walls stained with water marks. My father had neglected its upkeep, so preoccupied was he with his new life and family.

"Can't we fix this?" I ask Maman, pointing to the leak.

My mother does not respond and I understand. She probably does not have the money. My father's meager retirement money is split between his two wives. Other family property in his name has gone to his brother or to Afsaneh. We are left with this house.

"Maybe we should sell it," I say.

Maman does not want that. She will never again afford a home like this.

"It's a small leak," Maman says. "Just make sure to empty out the can."

On the street, Shirin waits for Maman in her car. They are off to another *dowreh,* where the widows smoke fiendishly and brag about their trips to Syria, Dubai, or Kuwait.

"Don't wait up for me," she insists as she leaves the house.

How will my mother even afford this simple life when I am gone? I have saved little from my translation job, slim savings that are quickly dwindling despite the favorable exchange rate of dollars to rials. Maybe it's time to return to the United States, to get another degree, to start a business. Or maybe I should launch my own translation business here. But where would I begin?

A flash of lightning brightens the sky for an instant as a tall man approaches the gate to our home.

"It's me," Hamid yells loud enough for me to hear him from the garage.

I open the front door to let him in.

"Do you mind?" he asks, and I shake my head.

He removes his soaking boots and raincoat outside the door but still drips water into the living room. His clothes are damp and he rubs his hands together for warmth. He grabs a towel from the bathroom to dry himself as I offer him tea, sugar cubes, and sweets. When he finishes his drink, Hamid walks over to the bookshelf and finds the Divan of Hafez. He flips through the tome and recites a passage about fate and love in a crisp, polished voice.

"Hafez is not easy to read," I say.

"And even harder to understand," he continues.

Then, quite abruptly, he asks, "Do you have matches?"

Hamid reaches for my father's water pipe on the console table and retrieves some tobacco and a piece of coal from his pocket. As he fills the *qalian* with the finest *tombaku* of Shiraz, I pass the matchbox to him. The tobacco he smokes with such equanimity was once the source of hidden pleasure, and of political protest, for the women of the shah's harem. Tonight, it is our gesture of silent rebellion. Smoke rises in the room as Hamid brings the pipe to his lips and inhales. Then he hands it to me. At first, I decline but he insists. The aroma is pungent. I suppress a cough as we share a moment of intoxication.

Hamid asks about my recovery, the ruptured spleen, and any plans to return to the United States. I don't know, I tell him. We sit quietly on the couch together. He puts his arm around me. This is an embrace I never sensed from him before—a touch of calm and tenderness—maybe even love. He walks over to the stereo and finds Persian folk music, simple paeans to love sung to rueful, bucolic melodies.

"Take me to the Caspian," I say.

"Now?"

I nod.

"What about your mother?" he asks.

"We can call her from your mobile."

He does not resist. I put on a raincoat that passes for a *rupush* and a beige headscarf and we walk to his car. As he starts the engine, he removes his vintage silver agate ring from his pinky and places it on my wedding finger. It fits loosely and almost falls off my hand. "In case someone asks," he explains. Before long, we are at the unmanned Karaj toll booth. The highway, shrouded in darkness, expands to three lanes. Only the headlights on the cars light the roadway. I place the CD of folk music in the player and turn up the volume. As we drive, we listen to a simple song about a peasant girl named Gilan, a beloved maiden whose name invokes the coastal beauty of the Caspian province.

At daybreak, Hamid winds through the olive groves of Rudbar, whose clay houses still bear the deep cracks and indignities wreaked by repeated earthquakes. When we finally reach his family's villa, the cypress tree sways gently with the seaside breeze. A turquoise gate opens into the garden and leads to the terrace. It was here that I had first met him at an elaborate luncheon thrown in his honor by his mother.

The caretaker, Ahmad Agha, hears the squeaking doors and approaches the terrace. He looks surprised to see Hamid. "We didn't know you were coming, sir," he confesses. "My wife hasn't made the beds." Hamid assures him that we can attend to our needs. The caretaker glances at me from the corner of his eye but does not dare to question my presence. The caretaker's wife, Robabeh, follows the cobblestone walkway and joins us on the terrace. She welcomes us and opens the door to the kitchen to prepare some tea. Ahmad Agha offers to buy fresh *sangak* bread at the local bakery, where the *naan* is cooked flat in a brick oven covered with pebbles.

I meander along the shore. The surging waves that threatened the coast with their vehemence have now tempered to ripples. A path of delicate sea shells emerges from the smooth sandy bottom of the sea. Peasant girls roam their gardens again picking fresh tomatoes and herbs to prepare the day's meals. Hamid gestures to me when Ahmad Agha returns with the *sangak* bread. I find my way back on the walkway leading to his villa. The gardener hoses down the interlocking cobblestones to wash off the sand that fills the gaps, but he shuts off the water when he see me approaching. His daughter, a mere toddler, finds a sandy surface and plays with her toy pail and shovel. For a moment, the blue plastic bucket seems to quiver but the tremors quickly stop.

"Here," Hamid says, "come sit at the table."

Near the entrance to the villa, the marble column sways anew. In unison, the antique crystal tea cups lining the ledges crash to the floor.

"It'll stop soon," Ahmad Agha reassures us, but the shaking chairs and wooden table belie his words.

"Run," Hamid yells, "run!"

Run where? There is no escape. I am caught between the debris of the column and the broken glass. I watch as the gardener's baby crawls aimlessly until Robabeh bends down to pick him up. I try to locate Hamid but can't turn my head. My eyes are shutting. When I look up again, I watch the dust of ages settle beneath my feet. It is at this stage, between oblivion and sleep, that I see them. Slowly, the whispers of lost prophets silence the lament of martyrs. When the chorus of a familiar poem repeats itself, I listen.

Martyrdom Street

Did you ever wonder why you were brought to this life?

I did.

Now I know.

We hold on tight to the hidden faces and climb high above the mountains and the trees. From the corners of Martyrdom Street, I smell the dust of a ravaged empire and its buried promises, and I know one day we shall show our faces in the land of Parsa, rising against tyranny.